CHRONICLES OF AETHERIA

Callum Arnold

Illustrated by Kimberly Arnold

Dear Benjamin,
I hope you like the book, it was an incredible journey. Life is a series of journeys, so take life one step at a time!

Copyright © 2014 by Callum Arnold
Illustrations copyright © 2014 by Kimberly Arnold

First Edition – February 2014

ISBN
978-1-4602-2060-3 (Hardcover)
978-1-4602-2061-0 (Paperback)
978-1-4602-2062-7 (eBook)

All rights reserved.

No part of this publication may be reproduced in any form, or by any means, electronic or mechanical, including photocopying, recording, or any information browsing, storage, or retrieval system, without permission in writing from the publisher.

Produced by:

FriesenPress
Suite 300 – 852 Fort Street
Victoria, BC, Canada V8W 1H8

www.friesenpress.com

Distributed to the trade by The Ingram Book Company

DEDICATION

To my friends, "Friendship has no survival value; rather it is one of those things that lends value to survival."
-C.S. Lewis

To my family, "You are not anything, you are everything."
-Michael J. Fox

Table of Contents

Dedication iii
Map of Aetheria vii
Chronicle One: The King's Conspiracy 1
    The Assassin 3
    The False King 7
    The Plot 13
    The Proposal 15
    The Nightmare 19
Chronicle Two: The Necromancer's Plot 21
    The Wraith 23
    The Spirit Rises 27
    The Unexpected News 31
    The Unforeseen Trip 37
    The Courtyard Battle 45
Chronicle Three: The Half-Blood's Hammer 51
    The Escape 53
    The Report 59
    The Impossible Task 63
    The Reunion 71
    The Downfall 77
    The Thief No More 81
Chronicle Four: The Gift of the Gods 87
    The Horde 89
    The Reluctant Return 95
    The Past Revealed 101
    The Memories Return 105
    The Trap 109
    The Visions 113
Chronicle Five: The Three Realms Unite 117
    The Redemption 119
    The Epic Battle 125
    The Sacrifice 135
Epilogue: That We Might Always Remember 143
    The History is Recorded 145

Map of Aetheria

Chronicle One: The King's Conspiracy

The Assassin

A hooded figure entered town on a black horse. He whispered to the beast as he dismounted and the massive creature galloped off in the direction of the forest. The fog thickened as he approached the local tavern. He wrapped his cloak about himself as he entered. If anyone had been watching outside, they would have perceived the glint of metal and the distinctive *snick* of a blade being drawn. No one witnessed his preparations. The man sat at the bar without so much as a glance cast at him. As the night drew on, men staggered home unsteadily until there were only three patrons left in the tavern: a swarthy man nursing his tankard in the corner next to the fire, a lanky, dark-haired man sitting at the bar wearing a heavy woolen cloak and a broad shouldered patron with a dark hood obscuring his face. From the corner another cup of ale was ordered, and at the same time the hooded man who was known among the villagers as Ezekiel Bright-Talon left his perch and took a seat further down the bar alongside his prey. Taking a long pull from his red wine he drew slowly closer. As he tipped his glass for another sip his concealed weapon was swiftly thrust into the abdomen of his companion. Heavy layers of felted wool soaked up any trace of the blood, leaving no clue as to the victim's fate. Ezekiel's target slumped over onto the counter with his head across his arms giving the appearance of one who has had too much to drink. At this point the bartender who had been wiping the opposite end of the counter and was eager to close up, noticed the prone figure and scowled. "Must be the ale," he muttered, and dragged the man towards the rooms of the inn to sleep off his troubles. As Ezekiel rose, a slight grin crept across his face, he exited the tavern and strolled in the direction of the forest. Ezekiel whistled shrilly, signaling to the king's guard that the target had been dispatched and could be disposed of in the morning.

A HOODED FIGURE ENTERED TOWN ON A BLACK HORSE.

The target was a cagey thief who had been causing trouble with the king's guard, and the job probably wouldn't fetch much coin for his purse. However, the king, who held a high opinion of himself and was rather pompous, was Ezekiel's most frequent employer. After seeking experience abroad Ezekiel had returned home to Aetheria and quickly heard the rumours circling around court. Information which explained how the king had grown up as the forgettable son of a rural nobleman, whose singular defining trait was his unquenchable thirst for power. Through years of plotting and preparation, he finally usurped the throne, by seducing the queen and forcing her into marriage. Unfortunately, the queen perished shortly after giving birth to Aetheria's new heir. The court physician deduced that the queen had ingested a rare poison. As a fitting turn of fate, the king had grown to love his wife and was heartbroken upon her death. Whereby he quietly cursed himself and his blind ambition for that fateful day before their wedding, the day he had struck a deal with a local thug to have her food poisoned. However, having gone to such lengths to win the throne, he was intent on keeping his crown. Thus, Ezekiel was called upon almost daily to accomplish all manner of tasks requiring more specialized skills than a castle guard or scholar possessed. Very few people knew about Ezekiel's past and he was happy to keep it that way. As a boy, he had been raised by his brother Kalleth, who taught him combat skills and how to write in six languages. Most importantly, Kalleth had taught him the virtues of a knight: courage, honour, humility, and the thirst for knowledge. Once Ezekiel had reached the age of manhood at sixteen years, he was given a coat of arms, bid farewell to home and was sent on a quest to find honourable work. Eventually he made a name for himself as a mercenary working his way across the realm until he had returned to Aetheria and found his way into the king's service. It was a fortunate turn of events indeed as his older brother Kalleth was already employed as advisor to the king. The passage of time had favoured the Bright-Talon brothers and Ezekiel was now approaching his eighteenth birthday at which time he would be able to marry and start his own branch of the family tree. Of course that would require finding a suitable mate. Ezekiel had always felt he had led a charmed life in many ways and perhaps fate would intervene in matters of marriage as well. He pushed those thoughts to the back of his mind for another day.

As Ezekiel reached the edge of the wood, he called out, "Returnos equinar!" (Return Horse!). He felt the familiar pulse of magic flow through him. There came a loud galloping sound and from the trees and in a flash of sharp yellow light appeared Ezekiel's horse, appropriately named Thunder. He mounted his charger and headed toward home.

As the king sat on his throne, he gazed at the door. "Where is Ezekiel?" he shouted at his guards. "We believe he is returning from the mission now Your Highness," said Kalleth, the king's most loyal advisor. "I saw him in the courtyard Highness, speaking with your daughter," exclaimed Mithros, captain of the king's guard. He then smirked slyly at Kalleth, his rival at court. The king's features rapidly turned the colour of a ripe tomato. His face contorted into an expression of rage which resembled a baby frowning. "Get Ezekiel NOW!" shouted the king. All of his attendants scurried out of the throne room. The king waited.

THE FALSE KING

Ezekiel rode quietly through town. When he looked upon the hard working Aetherians, farmers, trades people and merchants alike, he felt immense sorrow. He knew many of them personally, having worked with them at some point or other during his career serving the king. And even now, they were being abused by the king's decrees. He watched in surprise as a good friend of his was being forced to hand over money that was labeled as "taxes". Ezekiel scowled at the occurrence, knowing full well that the pouch of crowns would be contributing to the latest of the king's lavish expenditures. He approached the castle with its dark turrets looming in shadow. He heard footsteps from behind. Surprised, he turned in his saddle to see Tereleth, the king's daughter. "Your Grace, I..." he said as he searched for words. "Be silent", she whispered. She was very beautiful, with copper coloured hair and cerulean blue eyes. Her beauty, Ezekiel mused, grew with each passing year. Alas, it was doubly impossible for him to court her. She was not yet of age for marriage, and as the king's daughter a more suitable match would be carefully planned for her. "Oh brave knight," she pleaded, "please don't help my father! He is wicked and heartless. He cruelly plots to ensure royal bloodlines by marrying me himself!" Outrage burned in Ezekiel's heart at this proposed abomination. He bowed his head towards Tereleth and continued on to court. He had a few choice words for the king.

Slowly, the door to the throne room opened and with it a chink of light and the brave knight strode forward into the darkened room. The king chuckled. How fitting, he thought. "Why would an honourable knight," he began in a booming voice, "try to overthrow his king?" Ezekiel flinched and spoke, "Why not light a torch, so we may speak face to face?" At this the king chuckled and asked, "Why do you keep me in the dark about your dalliance with my daughter?" asked the king menacingly. "There has been no breach of trust on my part; your daughter approached me in the courtyard." Ezekiel began to step back slowly, his sense of foreboding grew into dread as he bumped into solid walls. "If there has been no treachery, then why are you attempting to leave?" asked the king. The next moment Ezekiel felt several hands grasp his arms, he was being dragged towards the dungeon. There was a bang and the crashing of armour, followed by the loud thud of bodies dropping. Suddenly, the torches flickered to life as Ezekiel strode into the light towards the dais and faced the king.

A single drop of sweat trailed down the king's forehead. "You would be called the worst of all knights, and killer of kings!" he exclaimed, trying to buy more time. "I would certainly undertake that task to ensure the safety of the kingdom!" shouted Ezekiel. The king stood up and unsheathing his sword cried, "Only I am fit to rule!". Ezekiel's eyes turned to steel, "Let us decide this matter in battle!" The brave knight and wicked king engaged in battle. Their swords clashed blow for blow. Several minutes passed, as the two warriors fought. Ezekiel grudgingly admitted that the king had grown adept at swordplay, however lax he was in other matters. They locked eyes when the king attempted a particularly ruthless lunge. Ezekiel saw in the man's eyes, a glow of malevolence that seemed quite familiar. He recalled a devastating event from his past when he had witnessed the same look in the king's eyes.

At the tender age of six, Ezekiel and his brother Kalleth were living on the streets, with no one to look out for them. On a searing August morning they were suffering terribly from thirst. An elderly woman took pity on them and gave them each a freshly filled water-skin. They both drank deeply and gratefully thanked the villager for her kindness. She simply smiled and waved goodbye. Feeling slightly less weary from the heat the boys carried on through town. At midday the brothers stopped and sat in the shade of an old tree devouring mouldy bread they had scrounged in an alleyway. Presently, a large crowd gathered on the street in front of the boys. They overheard many of the colourful comments made by the villagers who had stopped their work to watch the procession of the king and his royal guard. Ezekiel was spellbound as a glorious coach rode through town. Two snow-white stallions pulled the silken carriage through the clashing surroundings of dusty streets and mud coloured buildings. Ezekiel laughed quietly at the odd sight. Suddenly a scream sounded, and the boy had to climb up onto barrel to see what had caused the commotion. Ezekiel's heart wrenched when he saw that the elderly woman who had helped them earlier was now lying on the ground. As far as Ezekiel could tell, the horses had struck the woman as she crossed the street. The carriage's cream curtains parted to reveal the king, in all his splendour, although his black scowl diminished any appearance of grandeur. He yelled to his driver, "Why have you stopped knave? I'm already late!" The meek man replied hastily, "Your Majesty, a woman has been struck by the horses. I had to stop, or else we would run her over!" the king's face grew red. "Dispose of her immediately, and get moving!" He closed the curtains. The driver seemed indifferent to his instructions and he nodded to a pair of guards from the king's escort and they dismounted. The men marched toward the woman with a lethal finality. Before Kalleth could stop his brother, Ezekiel dashed through the crowd, dodging and weaving between the villagers legs, until he came to a stop at the woman's side. He stood before her, defiant in the face of the soldiers who towered over him. The guards observed him in silence, confused by the strange turn of events. The old woman smiled weakly at the boy's bravery and she was grateful for his friendly face, but she knew from past experience with the king that the boy's interference would only place his life in danger too. "You must go." She pleaded, "The king shows no mercy, and for me there will be no escape." But Ezekiel, brave as he was, stood his ground against those who would harm his friend. The king's voice rang out from behind. "What is taking so long! Let us be gone!" he opened the curtains once more, and as he exited his carriage, a murderous look shone from his eyes. He took in the bizarre scene that played out before him. A street rat defending an old woman. So this was the cause of his delay. All Ezekiel saw was a villain, whose eyes gleamed with an evil fire. "I admire your bravery, little pup, but it may be that your display of courage will limit your lifespan!" The king drew his jeweled weapon, much to the shock of the observing crowd. "Give up your fight, for you must see how pathetic you are." He swung his sword and landed a sharp blow to Ezekiel's face with the flat of his blade, which left a small nick on the boy's cheek. The king then kicked Ezekiel out of his way, and turned to face the injured woman. Kalleth quickly ran to shield his brother from the horrible truth that was about to happen, but the little boy would not turn away from his cruel foe. The burning light in the king's eyes still glowed in Ezekiel's memory. Even as Kalleth tore his brother away from the scene, Ezekiel could hear the collective intake of breath from the crowd as they watched the king's evil deed, which was followed by sound of a sword being sheathed, and then finally the pounding of hooves as the carriage moved on. Ezekiel couldn't stop the tears as they fell, as he stared blankly down at the empty water-skin, all dried up, not unlike his innocence.

Ezekiel's lapse in attention ended with a loud clang, as he was knocked back by the king's vicious kick, and they resumed combat. He still bore the small scar on his face from that day. The knight thought of the old woman, and many others besides, who had been wronged by the king, and his thoughts also turned to Tereleth, whose innocence had been threatened by her own father. He took in a deep breath, and let all the welled up anger and sorrow he felt envelop him, and he lunged at the king. The king laughed, and eagerly lunged as well. At the last possible moment, Ezekiel dodged to the side. His steel found it's mark as the king flew by. Ezekiel quickly disarmed the king. As the monarch lay dying, he did not ask forgiveness, only that his daughter be kept safe. To this Ezekiel replied, "She is the rightful queen and I will commit myself as her loyal servant for as long as she requires." Ezekiel towered over his enemy and silently watched the king's eyes narrow in hatred, as he cursed the name of Bright-Talon. The capricious monarch suffered from mortal wounds and as such there would be no time for vengeance. Abruptly the king's eyes widened and then slowly closed.

ABRUPTLY THE KING'S EYES WIDENED AND THEN SLOWLY CLOSED.

Tereleth sat motionless in her room, shocked by the events that had unfolded. She stirred, letting her hair down and shaking it into loose waves. Her living quarters, even though she had grown to hate them, reflected her status. Her room possessed broad windows which provided an exceptional view of the village surrounding the castle. Unfortunately, whenever she looked out at the world below she was reminded of the incredible suffering and poverty her twisted father had wreaked upon the kingdom. Homes which once had been well tended were now falling into disrepair, Tereleth could see young children sleeping on the streets and begging for food. Faces that once beamed with laughter and hope, now bore the burden of hunger and fear. Tereleth's brow furrowed as she recalled the many cowardly deeds orchestrated by her father. The worst offense had been carried out the day he had usurped her mother's throne. He was a brash stupid man and yet she could not comprehend her feelings of grief. "Why?" she said to herself aloud. "I know why," replied a voice behind her. She jumped and quickly turned to see Ezekiel, her knight in shining armour, standing in the doorway. "You're angry with your father, but he raised you and was the only father you've ever known. No matter what sins he committed in the name of power, he loved you and you were a faithful daughter." She growled in response, "That's hardly true, I hated that man!" Ezekiel stepped into the room, and with a wry smile leaned against the wall tapestry as he recalled what his brother Kalleth had once told him about their family. "He explained how our father had abandoned us before I was old enough to speak." Ezekiel swallowed recalling the suffering they had endured. "I too was angry and furious with him for leaving us. However, deep inside I couldn't really hate him for becoming sick and making poor choices." Tereleth looked at Ezekiel directly. She had been admiring the hardworking knight from a distance after he began working for her father. He was quite handsome. Yet, her admiration was now tempered by her revulsion towards his lethal ability. "Wh-why did you kill my father?" she asked. Ezekiel looked down, and shifted uneasily. "I admit..." he took her hands into his own, and gently kissed her knuckle. "When you told me of your father's plan to marry you, I lost all perspective on the situation. I was consumed with a thirst for justice, and now that I see I've caused you pain, I am doubting the impulsive nature of my actions." He turned away, with his head hanging in shame. Tereleth watched him depart and questioned why she had let the only man who had risked everything in his effort to protect her leave without her forgiveness.

The Plot

Tereleth silently squirmed in the royal throne room, trying to listen to the complaints of the nobleman calling for taxes to be lowered. Without a doubt, she had never been more bored in her life. The pale, thin man spoke in a low monotone with such a deliberately slow pace that she found her eyelids drooping dangerously. Having been brought up in a royal household, she was dismayed that the business side of royalty had become so dreary. She had in the past endured some monumentally dull sessions at court during her father's rule. However, in these mind-numbing moments she often occupied herself by observing the opulent surroundings. Gilded pillars sprouted out of the floor and curved into the ceiling, forming magnificent archways. Large paintings adorned the hall, depicting ancient battles and more recently, portraits of her father had been added to the collection. Tereleth felt a sense of awe and pride in learning more about Aetheria and its rich history as told through the oil paintings which depicted grand tales of adventure and glory. She continued observing the walls for a few more minutes, but was roused from her musings by a hoarse cough. She felt her cheeks grow hot, noticing the nobleman staring at her with consternation. "I'm dreadfully sorry Lord Magn-" She froze and grew silent as he withdrew a dagger from his boot, which glimmered with a sickly green tinge. Silently, the nobleman launched the blade with deadly accuracy. Time seemed to slow down; Tereleth saw the knife speeding towards her head. Without warning, a giant, shining figure filled her vision, and a loud clang sounded as the knife made impact against metal. Slowly coming out of her shock, the queen recognized that Ezekiel had come to her aid again. Blunt and twisted, the lethal dagger lay at her feet.

Lord Magnus of the house of Sturm ran quickly for the door, and Tereleth could see his light pallor and fear from across the throne room. Consumed by rage, the knight who had saved her life chased the noble and pinned him to a wall so forcefully that the polished marble ruptured into jagged cracks. Ezekiel withdrew his blade and pressed it against the nobleman's neck, drawing a small bead of blood. A cry escaped Tereleth's lips as she witnessed the violent capture. Ezekiel growled angrily, sheathed his sword, and punched Lord Magnus in the jaw, knocking him out cold. He began to storm out of the room, as guards flooded in to aid the newly crowned queen. "Ezekiel, wait!" she called out, rising from the throne. But the knight simply stalked out of the room, armour clanking faintly as he departed. Accompanied by more guards, her advisor Kalleth was red-faced over the treasonous act. "Your Royal Highness, are you all right?" he questioned. The queen noticed that he gripped his hunting bow with white knuckles. Tereleth somberly replied yes and collapsed on the dais, overwhelmed by confusion. She was not accustomed to senseless violence, but at the same time, she knew that Ezekiel had only wished to protect her. Another feeling swelled in her heart, a warmth that comforted her which she found soothing. "My Queen, shall I escort Lord Magnus to the dungeon?" a timid voice sounded to her right. She turned and nodded to Othmar, her messenger, and said, "Make sure that Lord Magnus is locked away in the most foul cell you can find." Tereleth seemed so preoccupied that Othmar quickly scurried away. From a few feet away, Kalleth examined his queen with interest. He thought her to be rather complex, and the advisor hid his grin at Ezekiel's private admiration of Tereleth. Ezekiel had been drawn to the woman's compassion and strong sense of duty. She was, Kalleth thought, a perfect compliment to Ezekiel, indeed their natures seemed very compatible. Kalleth busied himself with returning the throne room to order, intrigued by the day's excitement.

The Proposal

A cool breeze wafted through Tereleth's window as she gazed down on the castle grounds watching the sun set. Merchants closed up shop and the streets quieted, evening torches blazed. Tavern keepers opened up and raucous laughter could soon be heard echoing from the warm buildings. She turned her gaze to her room, lighting a candle and opening a book. As the night drew on, she grew sleepy. Words began to swim across the pages, bringing dreams and wonderful thoughts started to swell inside her mind, as her eyelids drooped. "Psst! Tereleth!" she was startled awake. The room was dark, the candle had long since burnt out. Her servant, Othmar was rather diminutive however his slight build was easily overlooked because he was so efficient in his work, his long and lanky legs aiding him in rushing about the castle carrying out her wishes. Othmar stood in the doorway, holding a taper and his ring of keys. "Erm, beg your pardon, Highness," the shy servant whispered meekly. "Milady, you requested I should wake you at this hour." Tereleth yawned. "Thank you, Othmar." She dismissed him and got dressed. Donning a riding cloak and high lined boots, she left her bedchamber and walked to the stables. Picking out a gentle walnut mare, she prepared the saddle, harness and reins and climbed aboard. Trekking through the forest, she followed a well worn path down into a small valley and arrived outside a cosy log cabin. As she arrived and climbed down from the tired mare, the first light of dawn was shining through the trees. A thread of smoke weaved above the chimney, denoting the presence of at least one individual. She opened the gate, and trod the stone path to the door. Knocking three times, she entered and the delicious smell of roast beef permeated the cabin. She sat down at the table, and helped herself to the hearty meal, sighing with a mixture of fatigue and contentment at the completion of her journey. "Good morning Your Majesty!" said Kalleth, entering the kitchen with a smile. He propped his hunting bow beside the cabinet and settled down at the table. "What brings you here?" A light entered his eyes, as he carefully observed her ragged appearance and the dark circles under her eyes. "Are you perhaps looking for Ezekiel?" Tereleth gasped at her royal advisor's accurate guess, and she nodded shyly. "Um, I was hoping to talk with him." The wise man laughed, and clapped his hands together. "Excuse me, Your Highness, my mirth is not at your expense. I am happy to tell you where he is, except that this morning, Ezekiel left in search of you at the castle!" He grew more serious, and stood up. "Your Highness, I would be happy to accompany you to back to the castle immediately, if you so desire." Tereleth smiled, grateful for her advisor's kindness. "That would be wonderful Kalleth, and thank you for the delicious roast beef." The archer's smile grew even wider as he blushed slightly, not used to receiving compliments. Kalleth uttered a word of thanks and led them both outside. Once saddled up, they rode back into the forest which was beginning to awaken with the sounds of morning. Finally the riders came to a stop on a high hill overlooking Autumn Castle. Moments later a black horse crested the grassy peak, and sitting astride the great beast, wearing his shining armour, and looking very gallant was Ezekiel Bright-Talon ."Kalleth!" exclaimed Ezekiel, as he dismounted, leaving Thunder to graze. He walked quickly over to his older brother and grabbed him up in a big bear of a hug. "It is good to see you, though our parting was brief." He glanced at Tereleth, and a mix of emotions flew across his face. "Ah," he bowed down, "Your Majesty." Tereleth sighed as he helped her dismount. Gesturing for him to take a seat, the young queen seated herself beside him on the grass. She carefully composed her thoughts before saying, "Ezekiel, it's all my fault. I..." she trailed off. Ezekiel with deepest respect in his manner pursed his lips and looked away. She placed her tiny hand on his elbow causing him to turn his face back to her. Ezekiel cleared his throat and said, "Your Majesty, may I speak freely?" she nodded her head with the slightest gesture, not even aware that she was holding her breath as she waited to hear what he meant to say, "Tereleth, I love you," said Ezekiel, "I think I loved you from the moment I first met you." Tereleth's face broke into the most beautiful smile as she let out a breath of air. She felt the same warm feelings in her chest, and they intensified upon hearing his declaration of love. Tereleth felt as though she had been set alight, and she removed the knight's helm. Tousling his hair, she said, "Ezekiel, I love you too." Kalleth looked away as the joyful couple kissed for the first time. He was uncharacteristically silent, almost meditative. A breeze washed over the hilltop, and with it came a peal of bells. Kalleth, puzzled, glimpsed a robed figure on the outskirts of the forest. Yet when he looked back, the figure had disappeared.

Meanwhile, the two lovers were absorbed in their new roles. Whatever magic had filled the air had helped the misunderstandings that had built up between them to disappear.

They continued to embrace and kiss as the sun rose high into the sky, and when at last they broke apart, Ezekiel knelt on one knee and pulled out a ring. It was simple, wrought of copper as bronzed as Tereleth's hair, and nestled in the center was a gem as red as her lips. "Tereleth, Queen of Aetheria, and my other half, whom I cannot bear to live without, will you marry me?" Tereleth sniffled, as salty tears filled her azure eyes and ran down her face. "Yes, I will marry you Ezekiel, my greatest guardian, you are part of me and I cannot fathom life without you. Yes, I will marry you!" They embraced and sat together on the hill for several more hours, enjoying the feeling of being together, whilst Kalleth watched out for them, feeling overjoyed that his brother had found love.

TERELETH FELT AS THOUGH SHE HAD BEEN SET ALIGHT.

The Nightmare

"I have watched your family for decades, Bright-Talon. Your pathetic exploits crushing villains can't hold a candle to the terror I inspire. And yet somehow, you continue to be a thorn in my side! I promise you this, Bright-Talon, Aetherian rivers shall run red with your beloved's blood, and I shall crush your brother's bones into meal! Everything you hold dear I shall pulverize with impunity as you watch, helpless to save them. Finally, I will bring you to the depths of hell and there you shall dwell forever more, at my beck and call!" Ezekiel sat up, waking in a cold sweat. He glanced over at his new wife, who was still peacefully asleep. He stood up and went to the balcony. The stars shone in the sky, points of brilliance in a black sea. He shivered, puzzled at the ominous nightmare that had woken him. He crawled back into bed, but even as he did he realized with utter certainty that someone, somewhere, was cursing his name and plotting to kill him and his family. He lit a candle on his bedside table, and muttered a warding spell. As he drifted to sleep, he heard a voice whisper, "I am the Necromancer, bringer of death, and bringer of sorrow..."

Chronicle Two: The Necromancer's Plot

The Wraith

A turbaned figure in flowing robes quietly entered the castle gate. The wind shrieked. The stalls creaked. The figure sprinted in the direction of the keep. A pale glow enveloped his body, and he became strangely transparent. As he slowed near the inner walls, he disappeared entirely, a wraithlike wisp in his place. The wisp crept up the wall, over the battlements and arrived at the base of the tower, pausing slightly, as if in thought. Then the wraith sped up and around the tower, floated beneath the balcony, and entered. Moments later a muffled cry disturbed the quiet night. A raven stirred and then flew off into the blackness. Some time later, a guard spied an apparition by the wall. He lifted his bow. His shot was true. The arrow pierced the glowing figure. The specter dashed off, leaving only a pool of its blood - a bluish-green liquid - and the chilling echoes of its evil laughter.

He lifted his bow, his shot was true.

The morning doves' sweet sounds awakened Ezekiel. "What a fine morning!" he thought to himself. As he dressed, a page knocked furiously on the door. "My

Lord! Kalleth, your advisor, is nowhere to be found!" Ezekiel frowned, "He is most likely at the market, do not worry over his absence." The page lowered his gaze and under his breath he muttered, "Very well Your Highness."

Tereleth sat on her throne, next to newly crowned King Ezekiel. Her face glowed with how good she felt having him at her side, helping to govern Aetheria. They were currently attending to matters of importance relating to the citizens of the country. A farmer was explaining the drought he experienced last summer and his need for extra loans. Ezekiel was tense for a reason she could not identify, and he'd been distracted all morning. The king's demeanor slowly darkened as the day went on. Surely, Kalleth should have returned by now, he thought to himself. Ezekiel's patience finally snapped. "Guard!" he barked. "Yes, my Lord! What do you wish?" the guard replied. "Find Kalleth for me before eight o'clock, and you will be rewarded with ninety gold crowns and fifty half crowns!" A gleam entered the guard's eye, "As you wish my Lord!" and he rushed off to seek his prize.

The Spirit Rises

"Rakvast gartnar Ishtvlack!" (Raise the earthbound corpse!) a voice chanted. The hypnotic tone rose and fell in a deep incantation, while a horrible moan was heard. Then suddenly, a bony hand with bits of flesh hanging off erupted from the ground and clawed at the dirt. This was followed by a fleshy arm, shoulder, and then a once human mass of decomposing flesh heaved itself out of the earth. As the skeletal fiend rose to its feet, it stood face to face with a bearded man. "You are Rakar, I am Svatan Alwyck Malic, your master." The man grinned, and the creature grimaced in return causing an awful crackling sound as bone and flesh collapsed and its jaw bone dropped to the ground.

As the guard searched the castle grounds, he saw several priests scurrying about the inner walls. When he approached, he noticed the cause of their distress. They were gazing dumbfounded at a puddle of pale blue substance. "What is the meaning of this Father?" the guard enquired. The priest frowned, saying, "I believe it is the work of Satan. The substance is both unnatural and unholy!" The guard, who was neither coward nor skeptic, was quite unsettled. Being the head of the king's guard, he began to question the relationship between the disappearance of Kalleth and the appearance of the puddle. However, lacking sufficient evidence, he continued inspecting the castle grounds for clues.

Kalleth moaned as he drifted awake. His head was in terrible pain. A rat crawled across his chest and clawed at his torn shirt. He turned his head, an act that caused him terrible pain. He gazed at the beam of gray light that spilled through the window. It illuminated a small patch of floor, upon which rested the hilt of his sword. He groped for the weapon, but succumbed to fatigue. He glanced to the heavens, praying for rescue as everything went black.

KALLETH MOANED AS HE DRIFTED AWAKE.

As the guard entered the inner keep empty-handed, his sense of dread grew at the possibility of Ezekiel's reaction. He strode into the throne room. Ezekiel's voice echoed through the hall. "What news do you bring me?" The guard gulped. "My Lord, I searched throughout the castle for Kalleth but no trace could be found." The guard paused. "I found a strange substance outside the inner walls which looked suspicious." The guard began to sweat profusely as memories of the previous ruler entered his mind. There were rumours that Ezekiel himself had murdered the king. His unease grew as Ezekiel remained silent. For several minutes he sat there unmoving, then rose to his feet. "Guard!" he said loudly. "Yes, my Lord?" the guard replied. He dreaded the thought of his punishment. "You have exhausted your efforts and failed to find Kalleth, but you are a strong and intelligent guard. You shall receive twenty quarter-crowns for your efforts. Now go, and serve your kingdom proudly." The guard could not believe his good fortune. He sighed to himself and said farewell to the king and departed.

Tereleth gave the subject of Kalleth's absence little attention, given that her brother-law was known to deliver messages throughout the kingdom. However, her husband grew more frantic as the day drew on. She caught up with him in the royal gardens, and after kissing him she asked him to sit down for a moment. "Ezekiel, what's wrong? Is it Kalleth?" The king sighed and joined her on the bench. "I am afraid my brother has been kidnapped. Kalleth was supposed to be here for council this afternoon and I know he hasn't been called to deliver any messages." He hung his head, deep in thought. Tereleth rubbed his back, and tousled his hair. "Go and find him then." Her husband looked up. "What?" She grinned. "Go find him, my love. I'll keep the kingdom running until you return." Ezekiel embraced her, and whispered in her ear, "I will come home, and when I do, you and I shall go to our hill upon where we first declared our love and we'll have a picnic." Tereleth hummed in contentment, recalling the balmy breeze that blew through the hills. "Farewell, Ezekiel." The knight king arose and caressed his wife's cheek. "Farewell, Tereleth." Ezekiel left the gardens, and searched out his manservant. "Nicholas, attend to me ." Ezekiel prepared a strategy for finding his brother and with a determined look on his face turned to leave, "Go to the stables Nicholas. Prepare Thunder and then go to the armoury and fetch my weapons and armour. I'm going on a little trip."

The Unexpected News

Tereleth watched as Thunder and Ezekiel disappeared into the forest. Her face fell as she turned to her manservant Othmar, "Ugh, I don't feel too well. Please bring some water to my room?" The servant bowed, "Of course, Milady." As Othmar scurried off, Tereleth made her way up to her bedchambers. She was turning the knob on the door when the nausea struck her full force. She rushed into the bedroom, past her bed and through into the water closet. After several minutes of vomiting, she looked up to see Othmar, carrying in her bucket of water. The Queen appeared very pale. She cringed with embarrassment, but nonetheless thanked him and requested the royal physician. While she waited, she lay in bed, trying to keep a piercing headache at bay. A short time later she heard a faint but persistent knocking . "Just come in already!" she snapped. The physician and Othmar leapt into the room with such speed that they tripped over each other and fell at the foot of her bed. She stared at them for a few seconds, and burst into tears. "What's wrong with me?" Tereleth sobbed, "I've been like this for a few days now, and I can't seem to keep any food down especially first thing in the morning!" The physician smiled knowingly, "You've been experiencing nausea, yes? Headaches, and I would suggest that you have been experiencing some shifts in mood?" Tereleth nodded, dotting the sheets with her tears. The physician nodded, "May I examine your belly, Your Majesty?" Tereleth obliged, lifting her shirt, for she was still wearing riding clothes from earlier that day. The doctor poked and prodded, now and then pressing an ear to her stomach. "Hmm," he mused. "Well, Your Majesty, I do believe congratulations are in order." Tereleth looked at the man in confusion. "For what?" The doctor straightened his glasses and gathered his tools. "It seems that, in all likelihood, you are with child and Aetheria will have an heir to the throne." Tereleth burst once more into tears, however, these expressed her joy at hearing the wonderful news. Othmar returned to the Queen's chamber. He had observed the whole roller coaster of emotions she had experienced, he asked with some degree of hesitation, "May I get you anything, Your Highness?" She looked up at Othmar, and smiled. "Yes, I have been craving strawberries for some time and now I know the reason. If you would be so kind as to find me some..." Othmar bowed, and promptly left before she could finish her sentence. She frowned at this bizarre lack of conduct, but shook it off, and stared at her stomach with newfound wonder.

"I HAVE BEEN CRAVING STRAWBERRIES." SAID TERELETH.

As Bruinen stood by the cauldron, he sensed a disturbance in the air indicating a new presence had arrived. He continued chanting over the brew, however he also added counter-charms to his chant. His staff glowed green in the roiling mixture. His tense shoulders relaxed at this sign. "Ezekiel, my boy!" he grinned and turned. "Tis I, potion master" Ezekiel said, with an air of reverence. "No need for such ridiculous formalities!" said Bruinen grinning. He stepped away from the cauldron and pulled out a chair. "Come, let us catch up old friend."

"It has been a while, little Talon," said Bruinen as he smoked his pipe in a chair. His silvery gray beard trimmed neatly, his robes pristine, it was hard to believe that this was the great Bruinen of old, whose power alone raised immense castles in days and leveled armies within hours. Ezekiel knew well the awesome power his mentor commanded. He had been witness to the wizard's powers many times, which gave him great respect for the man. "I have not been called that since I was but the tender age of seven!" gasped Ezekiel, confounded at the Potion master's sharp memory. "Ah, I believe it was the year that those scores of birds flew south before autumn?" Bruinen smiled at Ezekiel's expression. "Yes, and do you remember the events of that Friday in midsummer when it happened?" Ezekiel leapt to his feet. "Remember? I'll never forget!"

Bruinen straightened. "Refresh my memory," he said with eyes gleaming. Ezekiel sat back in his chair and recalled the events:

"It was Midsummer Eve, and all was peaceful. My brother Kalleth had just sent me to bed when, I heard steps behind me. I turned and saw nothing. I continued without another thought to the matter. I reached the house and entered. Some hours later, I awoke in a sweat. I lay in a clearing. There, in the shadows, were two blood red orbs. I stood up and the glowing orbs rose to eye level. They slowly came forward. Out of the shadows emerged a towering beast. Its muscular torso rippled with power. The jet black fur upon its back glistened in the moonlight. Its curved horns were sharp and blood stained. The creature rose to its full height. I was only five feet tall then. The creature must've been standing at the least ten feet tall, from the blackened hooves to the tips of its gnarled horns. I stepped back. It roared. The deafening sound echoed for miles. I drew my pitiful knife from my night robe pocket. The blade was meager in comparison to the creature's gigantic hammer. It growled one word: "Ignaros!" (Ignite!) The carved symbol of a drake glowed on its weapon. Flames ignited across the head of his ungodly Warhammer. The hilt was engulfed in pure darkness. The beast swung downward. The resulting shockwaves tore the nearby earth apart. I was thrown against a tree. I nearly passed out. As I lay there barely conscious, a figure shimmered into view. He bore a long oaken staff crowned by a large green emerald. The surrounding air was thick with green energy. The power appeared to come from the stone on top of the staff. A pale bluish ray of light encircled the man. The creature swung with terrible might. Before the blow connected, it was intercepted by the blue energy. The hammer was flung out of the monster's hand. A faint howl sounded as the blue light faded. The creature roared in outrage and charged towards the man. The Mage stabbed his staff into the open pages of a massive leather bound tome that lay open on the ground. A white light appeared along with the peal of bells. The creature screamed in pain and vaporized as if drawn onto the pages. That was when you approached the book and kicked it closed with your foot and I heard you say as I lost consciousness, "Blasted Souleaters!"

Days later, I awoke in my bed with you and Kalleth by my side. You had been hunting the last remnants of the Demonic Horde from the days of the Great War. Kalleth then explained how you were an Arcane Master. He also told me you had offered to teach me minor magic. You kept your promise and to this day those skills have kept me alive on many occasions.

A WHITE LIGHT APPEARED ALONG WITH A PEAL OF BELLS.

"Well, my boy, it seems you have a gift!" declared Bruinen as he stood. "I have heard the bards of kings tell epics of mighty gods and ancient heroes but, you have more talent than all of them put together! Your tongue is akin to gold!" He continued to make wide gestures with his hands and grinned repeatedly. He crossed the room and selected an ancient volume from the shelf. "Now let's see if you remember your runes." Ezekiel stood. Bruinen set the book on his desk. He leaned upon his staff. His eyes closed and he intoned: " Vargarosh Mithrak Ulkar!" (Expel Fiery Plume!) An emerald flame shot from his staff. Ezekiel tensed.

"Revelesar Barra Sprak!" (Conjure Shield of Lightning!) A yellow shield materialized. As the flame engulfed the shield, Bruinen rose from his staff and whispered, "Thrista Rocas Horricanos!" (Throw Hurricane of Stone!) A storm of debris exploded from the staff. At this, Ezekiel retreated. He raised his arms to fend off the attack. It never hit. He lowered his arms to a grinning Bruinen. "You are as competent as ever, but you need to keep your wits about you. Now, what is your business in coming to me? Surely your royal duties do not permit you such leisure for social visits?" At this Ezekiel's face fell. "Alas, two nights ago my brother Kalleth disappeared from the castle. However, the only evidence recovered from the abduction was a blue-green substance lacking odour, taste, and bearing no resemblance to any known liquid." Ezekiel shuddered as he recalled the event. "Ah my little brewmaster, you are quite astute," said the wizard, his brow furrowed in deep thought. "Do you have a sample?" "Yes I retrieved it from the outer walls," Ezekiel said as he laid the vial on the desk. The wizard's expression morphed into extreme horror. "Oh gods almighty!"

The Unforeseen Trip

"Alas, my friend, you bring dark tidings," declared Bruinen. "And you bear darker burdens." The wizard held the vial at a distance as one holds a soiled diaper. "This is blood from an evil more ancient than any I have encountered." Bruinen hovered over various tomes on his shelf. "Come friend, to the cellar." Ezekiel followed the wizard down the stone steps into a decrepit cellar. The air was humid and reeked of mould and mildew. The walls were overgrown with vegetation. Bruinen, still gripping the vial, leapt to a trapdoor. He opened it, revealing even deeper chambers. This continued for some time, after which Ezekiel guessed they'd covered several miles. They travelled quickly from room to room. Ezekiel thought he glimpsed a skull here, a rat there, and after a while he asked Bruinen, "How long does this go on for? Why exactly do you have such a large cellar?" At this Bruinen laughed and replied simply, "Patience." Ezekiel decided not to decipher what that meant, but soon enough they reached their destination. Bruinen's eyes gleamed, "My private collection". He spent several minutes looking over some dusty books which Ezekiel noticed were considerably moth-eaten. Bruinen then reached over to a book that rested on a rotten chair. This activated a mechanism which revealed a hidden compartment. Ezekiel groaned pathetically. "Hush little Talon. This is a security vault for my private atlas," Bruinen said, with a touch of annoyance. "Perhaps this is slightly cumbersome..." he muttered. The Mage withdrew a book which might have been confused with a brick, heavy and rough as it was. "Here we are. Wraiths." He read the definition to Ezekiel and turned the page to an illustration of a pale, skinny creature whose facial expression radiated pure evil. Bruinen studied the page for a couple minutes when suddenly a distant rumble dislodged a cloud of dust. "My house!" Bruinen cried. "Telaros Porfaros!" (Teleport Portal!)

He yelled. Just like that, Bruinen and Ezekiel disappeared from the underground library.

Ezekiel felt himself whisked away by the power of magic. He could no longer see Bruinen. Then, quite suddenly, he felt a great weight upon his shoulders. He fell heavily to the floor of Bruinen's study. He was not alone.

Kalleth moaned in pain. He had been tormented for several days now. At least he believed it had been several days. He didn't know why he had been taken, only that his tormentor was both terrible and cruel. He struggled to lift his eyelids. He remained in the cell. He rolled his head to the left. The weapon was no longer there. He felt a looming darkness approaching. Then he knew no more.

Ezekiel rose to his feet. He glanced about and could not see anything. However there was a faint light which filtered in through a small key hole. He could see nothing except a simple table upon which sat a sword. He reached for his weapon and found it was missing. In the same moment he had reached for his weapon, a voice like silk had whispered, "Not a good idea friend." Suddenly, a dagger pierced the sleeve of his tunic. He gasped at a burning pain running up through his arm. "Poison that," said the same voice louder now. Ezekiel's foggy mind struggled to understand his surroundings. Finally his reasoning clicked in and he could see by the light from the hole that he was locked in a wardrobe. A flash of light and the smell of sulfur announced the arrival of Bruinen whose powerful voice filled the room. "Be gone foul maggot! Cursed be you and your offspring and their offspring!" The other voice replied, "Okay! Don't get your knickers in a twist ya old geezer! I just wanted a couple a'-" The voice stopped abruptly. Silence echoed through the room.

"Hel-," Ezekiel never finished the word. He collapsed in pain on the floor of the wardrobe. He fought to stay conscious but slowly sank down...

"You're late" said the purple-robed lady.

Kalleth woke up, eyes bleary. "Where am I?" he muttered. All around him was forest and greenery. He then began to walk, limping slightly, until he reached a freshwater spring. Thirsty, Kalleth knelt and drank deeply but soon heard a crunch behind him. Kalleth jumped up and swiveled around reaching for the sword he lacked. Standing there, with arms crossed and scowling, was a woman garbed in purple. "You're late!" she exclaimed, with a voice that while harsh remained silky and melodic. Kalleth's brow shot up, "Whatever might I be late for?" The purple-robed lady stalked closer, staring at him intensely. "You are late for the giving of your gift." After saying this, she pulled out a small vial and sewing needle. "Kalleth, you are needed for the coming battle."

"How do you know my name?" Kalleth said, stepping back slowly. The purple-robed lady smiled, raising her hand. "How could I not?" Kalleth felt somewhat peevish as he fell to the ground unconscious for what seemed like the thousandth time. The last thing he heard was her laughter.

———•◆•———

"Wake up!" yelled a voice. Ezekiel jerked awake to find himself lying in Bruinen's house. "What..." An enormous pain in his head prevented him from speaking. He couldn't even think straight. "You are safe, my friend," Bruinen replied softly. To Ezekiel the sound was unbearable and he winced in agony. "That fiend poisoned you!" the Mage growled. "Who was the...Argh!...the fiend?" Ezekiel asked as he rubbed his temples. The old wizard bent down to retrieve a battered tome. Its pages were torn and bloodied. Bruinen's face softened almost imperceptibly. "The thief was a small time crook whose employer wishes me ill. No sane person would dare approach, let alone try to steal, an Accursed Atlas!" He turned, his face in shadow. "It is a book whose pages contain demons." Ezekiel stared in complete shock and staggered to his feet. "That's impossible!" Bruinen began gathering his things. "Indeed, that book held a demon of semi-god caliber, The..." Ezekiel stared, puzzled. Bruinen reached for his staff. "It's name is unholy, I shall not utter it, the name itself means *Nos Nethrakos Lycan* or Hell's Shadow. The thief's employer wishes someone's certain death. With a weapon like that, he shall not find it hard to accomplish."

———•◆•———

"Will you come with me?" Ezekiel asked Bruinen as he shouldered his pack. Bruinen grinned. "No, that thief made quite the mess, but you'll be hearing from me soon enough." Ezekiel sighed. "Any tips for demon-killing?" Bruinen raised an eyebrow. "If you find yourself fighting a semi-demon, you should cut your losses and run in the opposite direction!" Ezekiel mounted Thunder. "Wish me luck!" Bruinen nodded, "Fight hard, little Talon." Thunder galloped down the road. Ezekiel didn't look back but a single tear slid down his cheek.

Tereleth had been flipping through a whole host of books - encyclopedias, atlases, and others - stacks upon stacks of them. She read frantically, inspected page after page, glancing to and fro so swiftly that the candles threatened to extinguish. She picked up the next heavy volume and brushing off the dust she read the title, *Brutus' Index of Beautiful Baby Names*. Tereleth scanned every page absorbing all of the information she could find. She was searching for a name for the baby. Ezekiel probably would have a whole host of ideas. All of a sudden a thought occurred to the queen: *Ezekiel! I never did tell him about our joyful news, and he still had not returned from his mission!* Tereleth got up, her reading materials forgotten. Exiting the library, she ran through the courtyard while rain poured down around her. She entered the throne room briefly, thinking how lonely it now appeared.

A few hours later, Tereleth arrived at Kalleth's cabin. She carefully dismounted her horse, opened the gate, and knocked on the door. Surprisingly, somebody answered. However, she had no idea who the old man, wearing blue robes and leaning on a staff standing in the doorway might be. A look of curiosity twinkled in his eye. "May I help you?" Tereleth raised a brow, "And who might you be?" she questioned with skepticism. The man grinned, an expression partly obscured by his voluminous beard. "I am Bruinen, of the Bright-Talon family, a student of magic and other arcane forces. I'm going to guess that you must be looking for my nephews, Kalleth and Ezekiel, and I have reason to believe that Ezekiel is your new husband." Tereleth smiled, and nodded, "Yes, I have come looking for him, and by extension Kalleth, for he has-" The old wizard held up his hand. "Been missing for some time, yes." Bruinen finished. "Come inside, it's cold and damp out here."

They supped next to a roaring fire that night, Bruinen listening attentively to all that had transpired over the past several months that Ezekiel and Tereleth had been married, including the latest revelation that she was now expecting their first child. Bruinen was delighted at this news, yet at the same time he was troubled, and wouldn't answer her questions on the matter. "My understanding is that your husband departed for a dark and bleak place, which was where we assumed Kalleth has been emprisoned." She gasped, "Wait, Kalleth was kidnapped?" Bruinen nodded, "Aye, and his abductor is a fearsome individual indeed. I bid you return home as quickly as possible as his minions are nigh upon us, and if you don't return to the castle now, I fear there will be no salvation. I wish you best of luck, and remember that no matter the danger he now faces, Ezekiel is not alone. Godspeed Tereleth, and may your child be as much of a source of pride and inspiration as his parents!" He ushered her through the door, fingering a worn looking book bound in black leather. She mounted her horse and rode hard through the rainy forest at a frantic pace, which is why she didn't notice the bony arm that uprooted her from the saddle and tossed her to the muddy ground. A pair of green-tinted teeth that had seen better days grinned in the downpour. "Hallo lass, seems ya shouldn't be roamin' about at this time o' night!" the filthy mouth said in a heavy accent. Tereleth was quickly tied up and then grabbed roughly around the shoulders and unceremoniously dumped onto the back of a pack mule. She was gripping the saddle with white knuckles when her captor suddenly placed an old corn sack over her head. Staying aboard the choppy mule required all of her strength and focus. Tereleth had no desire to fall off, as she feared this criminal did not seem like one who would right her should she lose her grip.

While they spent many hours on the road, Tereleth worried over what might happen to their realm with both the king and queen missing. When at last they arrived at their destination, the villain removed the dusty sack and Tereleth gratefully filled her lungs with large gulps of fresh air. She was led over to a tree, and securely tied to the wide trunk. A derelict bunch of bandits were squatting in the grove, and it seemed that they'd been there for some time. Tereleth caught her breath as she was approached by another man who she assumed was the leader of the band. He examined her with a critical eye, making her cheeks grow red. "Oy! Henry, come over 'ere!" he said, drawing his dagger. Her captor drew near and his leader glared at him, looking very angry indeed. "Say, Henry, do ya know who this lass is?" Henry stared blankly at Tereleth without expression. "I dunno, some lass I found south of Autumn Castle, she 'ad a nice horse she did, but the mare was galloping like the devils were chasing after her, and I only caught this girl. She's quite the looker though, ain't she?" The leader slapped him with the back of his hand, face red with rage. "It's the bloody queen mate! Haven't you been down to Autumn Castle lately? She's been the talk 'o the town! Usurped her murderous father she did! And you bring her straight into our hideout?" He kicked the dirt with obvious frustration, however his foul mood subsided as he studied his new prisoner. Wordlessly, he crouched down next to her and ran the edge of his blade down her cheek. A white scratch was proof that the man's hands were precise, likely a result of honing his craft over the years, picking pockets and locks alike. "We'll fetch a pretty penny thanks to you, Highness," he cackled, his foul breath making Tereleth gag. The leader departed, and she fell into a deep exhausted sleep.

A silhouette against the dark sky. A blight of blights. A curse upon curses. That is what I am, thought the skeletal form of Rakar, as he watched over the prone body of Kalleth. Svatan, his master, had instructed him not to let Kalleth leave this cell. Poor use of the undead as far as he was concerned. Charged with guarding a weak human, he mused. Kalleth moaned. Rakar gazed up, curious. Kalleth's lips barely moved as he whispered "Need water, so thirsty...have some?" Rakar's raspy voice chuckled, "My dear sir, you won't be needing water where you're going." Kalleth surged up from the ground with unexpected ferocity. His hands grasped for the monster's neck. Rakar swiftly ended the threat of attack with his fist and a blow to the prisoners stomach. Kalleth, doubled over in pain, grinning as he fell, for his distraction had created enough time to attack his captor. He had driven the poisoned shard into the zombie's neck. Rakar's reddened eyes rolled back into his head as he tumbled to the ground. Kalleth was going to have to figure out a way to thank the mysterious woman from his dream. The shard and poison she gave him had somehow manifested into reality and the tools had worked perfectly to neutralize his creepy guard. Rakar's body was instantly paralysed even as his mind watched the prison break in disbelief . Kalleth reached for the keys. Success! He rose swiftly to his feet, and rushed off in the direction of the armoury.

Thunder's hooves clattered down the gangway. Ezekiel unclasped his hood which floated down to the ground. The sun was just touching the horizon. The barkeeper in the village had said he'd seen the wraith sail from this port. Now it was just a matter of tracking them, but how? He thought. He dismounted his horse and leaned against a post, making little waves with the toe of his boot. He looked up in surprise. *Waves! I could use a spell to sense the currents perhaps?* That would require very powerful magic but it couldn't hurt to try. Ezekiel sat down on the dock and lowered his head in concentration, his brow furrowed. He drew upon his reserves of energy, as Bruinen had taught him so very long ago. "Now, you must be careful of just how much energy you use, for your power could be easily sapped by this level of spell, leaving no reserve energy for the attack. So use magic carefully," Bruinen's voice echoed in his head. He reached out with a hand and touched the water. He could sense all its currents, from the largest waves, to the smallest eddies. He reached back, to two weeks earlier, to a time when a small dinghy had left port heading northeast towards a mysterious island cloaked in mist and smelling of decaying flesh and sulfur. He opened his eyes and turned to face Thunder. "You're not going to like this."

———•◆•———

"Who goes there?" a deep voice rumbled. Ezekiel, disguised in dark robes approached. "Your master, Lord of Darkness." The voice chuckled, the ground started shaking. "You are not my master." Ezekiel drew his sword which was called Varkath. Ezekiel shouted, "*Ignaros!* So be it." As he thrust his blazing sword through the air, piercing the blackened portal of the fortress. "Arrgh!" the voice roared. A chill wind permeated the area, rustling the dead trees. Ezekiel strode forth into the mouth of the blackness.

The Courtyard Battle

Kalleth groaned. *Not again.* He gazed at the mass of guards blocking the door of his prison. The lead guard growled, "Get him!" Kalleth raised his rapier. With swift strokes he cut down all twenty men. As he retrieved yet another set of keys, he sighed, "I'm getting too old for this." He continued on. Once he had reached the armoury, escaping the guards had been child's play. None had yet bested him in combat. He entered the courtyard and found himself surrounded by archers. "Ah, a challenge!" He fell into his defensive stance. "Surrender or die!" cried one of the guards. Kalleth grinned, raised an eyebrow and whispered, "Die." Every soldier fired an arrow. "For Aetheria!" Kalleth yelled. He leapt into the air, vaulting towards the gate, swept his rapier through the air, and flipped forward. Seven arrows found their mark. Kalleth tumbled down. Several soldiers continued to shoot him until the captain yelled, "Enough!" Calmly he strode forward, and in one swift motion, stabbed Kalleth in the chest. At that precise moment, all hell broke loose. Ezekiel charged in seated upon Thunder, who was garbed in full battle armour. Hordes of soldiers, dead and alive, streamed through every possible entrance. Kalleth, who lay in the center of it all, blood flowing freely, began to glow. As Ezekiel fought to protect Kalleth, he watched in amazement as the arrows slowly exited from his body, his wounds knit back together, and he began to heal. Thunder screamed and reared up. Suddenly everything stopped. All was quiet.

"Ahahahaha!" Svatan entered the courtyard, still chuckling to himself. He looked as though a harsh sun gleamed high above him, such were the depth and length of the shadows which fell upon his face. His eyes were searing with hot fury yet chilling in their cold cruelty, and his arms were lean and powerful. A pale fog surrounded him, and even as he approached, the few soldiers still living were abruptly asphyxiated by the deadly fumes, and almost instantly they were reincarnated into undead creatures. The necromancer was devilish in every manner, as if he had become one of the many monstrosities that crowded into the place. He smirked and raised his hand, letting a purple dust float to the ground. He placed what Ezekiel recognized as pages torn from Bruinen's Accursed Atlas on the ground and began to chant. A chill wind blew through Ezekiel's hair. A great quaking ensued. The earth roared and creaked. A great tear ripped through the middle of the courtyard. Several soldiers fell down into the abyss. A fleshy hand rose from the ground and gripped the edge of the crevasse which had formed in the courtyard. A mighty roar pierced the eardrums of all who were present. Hell's Shadow was rising.

Hell's Shadow was rising.

As Kalleth fell to the ground, he feared this was the end. There was an odd sucking feeling, and then an extraordinary sensation of lightness. A peal of bells sweeter than any he had heard before echoed in his ears. Then, as if from a distance, he saw a falcon land upon his breast. "Kalleth," a warm voice uttered, "You shall not die today." And so it was that he rose, without so much as a scratch, to find all hell converging upon him and his brother.

———•◆•———

Nos Nethrakos Lycan shook the ground with its cries. It raised its head in rage. The shriek that emanated from the beast was deafening. Several of the soldiers' ears began to bleed. A wisp of smoke floated up from the still fuming crack in the earth. The smoke brought with it a weapon: the demon's hammer, Ignaros.

———•◆•———

Ezekiel positioned himself back to back with his brother. "To the death?" he yelled out. "To the very end!" replied Kalleth. Ezekiel spotted Svatan slinking into the shadows, looking frightfully at the gigantic monstrosity towering above them all. He was astonished to realize Svatan feared the demon, even though he was responsible for summoning the beast! Then the first wave of undead soldiers engulfed them. Ezekiel stabbed, parried, and lunged with the precision that only experience grants. He knew that one mistake would be his last. Behind him, Kalleth fought with equal lust for battle and just as much skill.

———•◆•———

The battle raged on for what seemed like hours, for each enemy who fell, another rose to take his place. Despite the demon lord's raging, he had begun to pay greater attention to those around him. Several soldiers who had stabbed at him in fright now hung from his gaping maw. Ezekiel could tell that Kalleth was growing tired and he knew it would not be long before a miserable fate would befall them all. In a desperate act of faith, he drew upon his energy and used the strongest spell of summoning he knew. "Bruinen Varos Mene!" (Bruinen Come To Me!) he roared.

———•◆•———

Hell's Shadow, the unearthly being whose thoughts had been jumbled and cryptic, suddenly came into sharp focus as he overheard the words of the summoning spell. *Power. Master has Power...* "Raargh!" The creature started to move its ancient limbs. Massive joints creaked and huge muscles strained and stretched in order to move after being confined. The demonic creature slowly began walking toward the maelstrom that was raging in full force. Ezekiel and Kalleth had fallen and were now held at sword point by the entire undead army. Svatan's Army had won.

Chronicle Three: The Half-Blood's Hammer

The Escape

A lone guard walked the halls, bored beyond imagination. He twirled his keys on the index finger of his left hand distractedly, thinking of the hunk of roast ham his wife had sent for lunch. He swallowed hard and tried to ignore his grumbling stomach. The watchman was deeply lost in thought, when he spotted a big rat scurrying across his path. Terrified of rodents, he jumped in fright as the keys flew from his hand onto the floor. Stooping to retrieve them, the guard was suddenly struck heavily upon the head. As the guard tumbled to the ground, a skinny hand nimbly snatched up the keys. Soon, a multitude of feet were heard padding throughout the prison, as all of the captives were released to create a suitable diversion. Only one pair of feet however, chose to exit by way of the roof. Their owner had carefully noted the schedule of the guards patrolling the jail. By dawn all of the prisoners had been recaptured and brought swiftly back to their cells. All except for the thief known as Verin Elhadhir, also known to the prison population as Silver-Tooth, a nickname which he owed to the mischievous grin that crossed his face as he cut the throats of his victims when he stole their lives and money. Of course, these were just rumours, untruths spread by Verin himself to breed fear and prevent unnecessary trouble or interest in him while he was incarcerated. In reality, the reason for his imprisonment was his incessant harassment of the king's guard and the royal coffers which he was chronically attempting to lighten. Oh, and his cynical attitude, love for precious gems, and his latest attempt to fulfill his father's wishes by stealing a sacred staff certainly hadn't helped his case. After managing to avoid capture from his successful prison break Verin thought it best to try to blend into the village and lay low before making any move to return to his father.

Unfortunately, the king's men had found his local cache of goods and had laid a trap waiting for his return. As such, his money and most of his clothes had been confiscated. A stolen farmer's cloak would have to suffice. Verin had been laying low at the tavern for some time, hoping for the excitement from the prison riot to die down. "Ye be needin' some warmer clothes lad?" the barkeeper asked, with a raise of his brow. "No, I'll just be having some Briarheart ale," Verin frowned in annoyance. The hooded man on his right, who'd emitted a sinister aura the entire evening, was inching towards him with snakelike precision and silence. Then, in a sudden flurry of movement, Verin was stabbed in the abdomen. His head slumped onto the counter. He was barely conscious as the stocky barkeep dragged his body towards a bedchamber in back of the tavern. Verin thought he heard a whistle but the darkness soon swallowed him up. In the morning the owner had flagged down the king's guard to have them remove the young lad's motionless body as he complained about the number of vagrants that darkened his door of late.

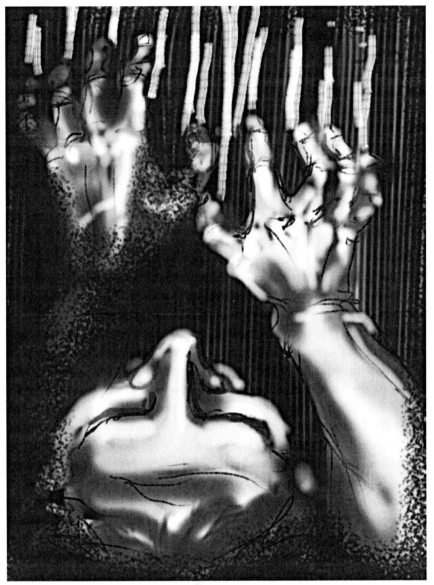

HE'D BEEN BURIED ALIVE!

Verin gasped awake and felt his lungs burn as they craved deeper gulps of air. He woke to pitch-black silence. He tried to sit up and banged his head. *Uh oh*, he thought. He slowly raised a hand and felt cool hard wood beneath his fingers. He'd been buried alive! He began punching at the pine box lid and tried yelling as loudly as he could. Dirt flooded his face, rocks pelted him constantly and it took all his strength not to breathe in. The wood, tough though it was, began to crack inward. Verin took a huge breath, and burst out into the ground. The hard cold chill of the earth surrounding him was more smothering than any amount of darkness. He emerged in a neglected graveyard filled with ancient tombstones.

Verin turned around to find a tombstone with his likeness carved into it, along with the phrase, "The king sends his regards." He clenched his fists as he felt a horrible hunger take over. He looked around and spied a deer grazing in a thicket a short distance from where he stood. His voice, clear but hoarse from his recent ordeal, rang out. "Laeraus Rochas!" (Launch Stone!) The deer dropped dead, temple crushed by a small rock.

Verin sat by a roaring fire and imagined hundreds of ways he would torture his assailant from the tavern, when something caught his eye. He looked over at the cemetery. A lone figure was bent down on his knees, gazing into the hole Verin had just vacated. Yet, here he was sitting in a clearing across from the cemetery, disheveled, misshapen and in plain view, and the stranger questioned none of it!

At that moment, the figure approached him, slowly but surely drawing nearer. As the figure crossed into the firelight, a wide grin spread across Verin's face. "Brother!" He shouted as he hurried to embrace the turbaned figure with open arms. "My, you have grown, Dazra my lost little brother!" the richly enrobed figure smirked. After grabbing a seat by the fire Verin chuckled and nodded, he still suffered the ill effects from being buried, "My time here has been interesting indeed. You must remember I am called Verin on the earth plane dear brother. Tell me, Alwyck, how is father?" At this, Alwyck became solemn and very quiet. "He requests you return and give him news of the mission." Verin paled and withdrew from his brother's scrutiny. "What is it, Dazra? mm sorry...Verin is it? You look quite ill." His younger brother sighed looking rather sheepish. "Father's mission has proven too difficult for me to accomplish. The mortals are vigilant." Alwyck raised an eyebrow, turning and said, "Very well." They both knew that as high level demons they could use black magic to effectively accomplish anything on the mortal plane. The look that passed between siblings acknowledged a stalemate of sorts. Somehow the brothers knew that each was keeping deeply hidden secrets from the other. "I must warn you Verin, Father will not take kindly to your failure." Alwyck departed and Verin was left to his half-finished deer on the spit.

Verin awoke with a start. He had dreamed fitfully of horned monsters and biting steel. He gazed moodily into the smoldering fire and then without any discernible movement, the fire was snuffed, his pack sorted, and the deer's remains wrapped. He rose to his feet. Without a backwards glance, he set off into the woods.

He is Weak! thought Zarym Malic.

The Report

Alwyck stood brooding as he waited for his father's next command. His mind drifted to a recent conversation he had held with the high ruler of the netherworld, Zarym Malic, over his choice of suitable appearance. Yes, his father's preferred form was that of an ancient minotaur. "Dreadfully out of style!" Alwyck had insisted, "Adapting the guise of a monster was a sign of the old ways!" he had scoffed, and then gone on to say, "Father, these days, you want go for more subtle, and bizarre guises, not the 'I just stepped out of a history book' look!" Alwyck shivered slightly as he remembered that the conversation had not ended well.

His eldest son's fashion opinions aside, the disgruntled father sat on his throne and stewed over the current predicament of his second son, Dazra Malic. He had just received a full report from Alwyck on the current status of his youngest offspring who was traipsing about the earth plane calling himself "Verin" of all things, which was a total dig at his father for his mistreatment of the brat's mother, Averina Bright-Talon, who had been an enchanting but fragile mortal woman.

He is weak! thought Zarym Malic. His blackened horns gleamed, and his fur glistened with a dark sheen as his barely contained temper boiled. The only noise breaking the strained silence was that of his hooves stamping in irritation.

Zarym Malic was a formidable demon of ancient renown. His kin were all incredibly powerful. Rumours told the story of a time long ago, when Zarym Malic had fallen under the spell of a mortal woman. Unfortunately, their twisted union had created a Half-blooded son. Over time it became clear to all in the nether realm that this second son could not live up to his father's expectations. Dazra Malic had continually demonstrated weakness of character. Physically, however, the hybrid lineage made Dazra stronger and more resistant to the harsh cold of the earth. The child's weakness, it seemed, stemmed from his human morality. Dazra questioned even the simplest order, and ruminated upon such trivialities as honour, justice, and - inferno forbid - kindness! Zarym Malic snarled in fury at the incongruity; perhaps the boy's only good trait was his lust for riches. Unfortunately, even that was tempered by the youth's misguided theory that the poor deserved to know wealth. It was bloody ridiculous!

In a cold fury Zarym Malic had sent his youngest son, Dazra, to the human realm to retrieve an artifact under the pretense that the power the object held was being used by an evil lord to cruelly abuse his slaves. Dazra, being at first skeptical, had agreed to carry out the mission. However, once the job was at hand Dazra had guessed his father's true intentions. Zarym Malic sought the artifact for himself as the sacred staff could be used to create a cage of concentrated energy which the demon lord planned to use to unleash natural disasters and wreak havoc upon the earth plane. Much to his father's disappointment, Dazra quickly abandoned his father's decree and adopted the guise of a thief named Silver-Tooth and set out robbing various kingdoms to appease his father.

However, after several years passed, Dazra finally returned to the nether realm only to discover that his father had been imprisoned by a great wizard using an Accursed Atlas. Seeking to explore his newfound freedom, Verin, as he preferred to be called, had returned to his lair on the earth plane only to find a contingent of the king's guard waiting to trap him. He had managed to think fast enough to find a suitable escape route.

Yet even as he reached the crest of the hill, Verin realized quite abruptly that he was lost. The sun was setting and the sky was darkening. He sprinted down the hill searching for a tall tree to prepare his nest for the night. A branch snapped. Verin glanced back and tripped on a root. Towering above him was a massive wolf. A low, guttural growl rose up from deep within its chest. The sound slowly rose in pitch until it ended as more of a yip. Verin stood slowly and took a step back. The wolf also paused as if to pounce, and then suddenly withdrew into the thicket, lost amidst the many other eyes staring out into the dark night. Verin continued on. While he walked, he gazed absentmindedly at the massive trunks of the pine trees, pondering his flawed family relationships.

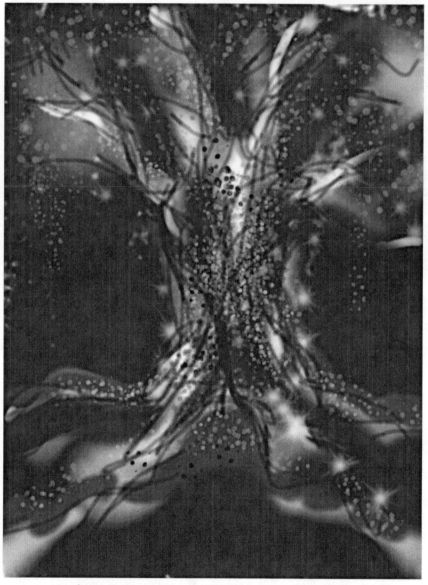

A local baker had bragged about an enchanted grotto.

The Impossible Task

Memories flooded into his mind. As if watching himself from a distance, Verin let his mind recall the painful past he could never really escape. He pictured a younger version of himself wandering through the forest with no particular destination in mind. "Why must you be so elusive?" he thought peevishly as he searched for what apparently didn't exist. His father had sent him into the corporeal plane to find precious materials that would be used to bribe mortals into his service. A local baker had bragged about an enchanted grotto which revealed itself at dusk and contained great riches. Thus far, Verin had failed to locate it. Several hours of careful searching had failed to yield any sort of configuration that might house a mysterious grotto. As he tramped through the forest, reflecting on these facts, he stumbled over a root. Falling heavily, he grumbled as he got up and brushed the dirt off his tunic. He gazed over at the root and conjured a lower level demon of sufficient strength to dispose of the culprit tree. When Verin looked up he cried out in shock, "Wait a minute!" The root that had tripped him belonged to a tree which had a large hole in its trunk. Verin crept over to the tree and with great caution peered into the darkened hole whose peculiar shape and size might have once been home to an animal. He could faintly hear the sound of rushing water, which piqued his curiosity. The dark fissure in the tree revealed nothing. In that moment he looked over at the Atronach, a demonic servant, who floated idly next to a bush, incinerating ants out of boredom. "Helius," Verin said using the language of the netherworld. "Explore this crevice swiftly and return to tell me what mysteries lay within." The Atronach looked up and said in an amused tone, "Aye m'lord." Helius then shot into the hole, quick as lightning, leaving a smoking ring imprinted in the earth above where he had hovered.

After some time Verin, who was called by his demon name Dazra Malic in the nether realm, heard a whooshing noise which indicated his rapidly approaching Atronach. He knew this sound well; in his father's court there were many servants. Only high level demons used Atronachs as servants and messengers, for they were tedious to summon. However, these lower level demons were more useful than Imps, and were nearly as resilient as Djinn. Atronachs were also commonly used for cooking as well as scouting. As Helius shot from the oak tree, Dazra noticed a long slash on the demon's left tentacle, and numerous thorns were embedded in his body. "What happened?" Dazra exclaimed. "My lord," Helius replied, short of breath, "Do not enter! There are numerous defenses in place which grow ever more fierce the deeper you travel. Worse than that, I sensed a Lich!" The Atronach doubled over wheezing, and then abruptly dissolved as it returned to the demonic realm. A Lich? Dazra thought, *It would be next to impossible to defeat such a vicious foe!* He crept over to the opening, searching for any sign of the horrors Helius had mentioned. What mystery lay within that would warrant such heavy defense? Indeed, there was little in the universe that would require such powerful protection. "I know of only one artifact that would command the protection of an undead high wizard, known as a Lich." Dazra peered into the dark tunnel. "The ancient war hammer named Ignaros!" Surely such a powerful item would be worth the effort required to retrieve it. Dazra rose, and then let himself dissolve into the chaotic energies of the Demonic Realm.

"Gah, damn this sludge!" Dazra cursed, while he trudged through the dank and murky tunnel. Several hours passed since he had discovered the silver maple. He had sent a message via his Atronach to notify his father of his plan and he was now facing one of his greatest challenges. "Well, really, calling this an enchanted grotto was extremely generous, it would be more aptly described as an underground swamp!" Malodourous at this point, he was silently cataloguing the list of offenses he had endured: he had twisted his ankle, torn his cloak, was not sure what was running down into his eyes, and was already more filthy than a Grunge Ghoul, which was hard to accomplish. The proverbial icing on the cake was that Dazra was beginning to shiver. A supernatural side effect from the guardian spells he guessed. The tremours brought with them a feeling akin to the way in which humans feel fear. It must be said that spectral beings like Dazra were almost immune to fear, so one can imagine how unsettling the situation had become. Dazra was on the point of halting his search and turning back when he heard a slight click. It was then that he was violently flushed down a hole, which he could only imagine led deeper underground.

When Dazra finally hit the bottom of the chute, he began to feel slightly nauseated. The stench was unbearable, and despite having an iron stomach, he didn't think he could take any more long falls or foul odours. He trudged onward until he reached a large cavern. Massive stalactites marked the enormous cavern, water poured from numerous crevices, and thousands of bats could be seen nesting high above in the obscured ceiling. Near the back of the cave there was a pool which fed a whole system of streams trickling in all directions. "Grrrr..." something growled in the darkness. Dazra leapt back from the cavern. *Where is the hammer?* Dazra thought confused. He peered into the cave cautiously, "No sign of the Li-". His thought was cut off by a blow to his back which sent him flying through the air. He slammed into the wall and dropped like a rag doll into the pool. Dazra felt darkness closing in as he lost all consciousness.

Everything seemed to come slowly into focus as if he was waking from a dream. *That blow was incredible!* thought Dazra as he dragged himself from the spring. He looked up, eyes widening as he saw the Lich, a spectral phantom, wielding Ignaros, the flaming war hammer. Suddenly, as if by a tidal wave, he was crushed by a throng of monsters, demons, and fiends of all description that came pouring out of every hole, crack, and fissure in the cavern. He had been wondering where the monsters were hiding when he had investigated the grotto earlier, and now if he wasn't careful he would pay the ultimate price for his ignorance. All hell converged at once upon Dazra. He closed his eyes as he drew on the black magic in his blood and cast a banishing spell. "Narcos Vhairnouros!" (everything must perish) The cavern was awash with a green, sickly light, as all the monsters were consumed by the earth, sucked down between dimensions into the nether-realm. "Does this please you Father?" Dazra yelled and his voice echoed through the cavern. Zarym Malic's eerie voice permeated the air, "Yesss, feed me!" In response Dazra scowled, "You shall receive more before the day is up, Father."

Dazra turned to face the Lich, glaring viciously, "Give me the war hammer and your death will be quick and painless." The Lich snarled, "Never." Dazra sighed, "So be it." He charged full throttle towards the Lich and launched a powerful punch directly at its ugly face. The Lich flew into the air, arching awkwardly and then the creature slammed heavily into the damp earth. Astonishingly, within seconds the undead fiend clawed back up into a standing position and shrieked in outrage. Thrusting the massive war hammer in the direction of the threat he blasted Dazra and knocked him headlong into a stalagmite. "You want to play dirty?" yelled Dazra. "I can play dirty too!" he shouted and then quickly melted into the ground. Suddenly, a massive fist erupted from the earth and wrenched the Lich off balance, casting the brute high into the air. "I ask you once again," Dazra's disembodied voice commanded, "give me Ignaros!" From the crumpled heap that was the Lich came mocking laughter which grew louder as he pulled himself back up into a fighting stance. "I cannot feel pain you fool!" cackled the Lich. Dazra made no reply. *Boom!* The sound echoed faintly off the cavern walls. *Boom!* The noise grew louder. *Boom!* Still closer. *Boom!* The Lich began to shiver. *Boom!*

A gigantic wave crashed into the cave, and with the raging tide came the Minotaur, Nos Nethrakos Lycan. A great cacophony of sound was heard as the cave began to shake violently. "Father, help me!" Dazra cried, Nos Nethrakos Lycan slowly lowered his gaze, "You have failed me," the voice boomed. Dazra watched in horror, as the waves engulfed him.

Dazra was startled awake from the dark torpor which had consumed him after striking his head on the rocks and falling unconscious into the pool. As the fog in his head began to clear, so too did the nightmarish dream that had featured his death at the hands of his father. In reality, the Lich had chained Dazra to a stalactite, and he was now dangling high above a sheer outcropping of spikes. "Gwahahahahah!" jeered the Lich. "I believe you will make a tasty kebab!" the creature said as he motioned to the spike littered floor. "Perhaps we'll turn you into a roast!" Now it was Dazra's turn to laugh, "Fool, I cannot be consumed by fire!" The Lich's brow shot up as it conjured a perfect sphere of purple fire, which radiated a bone-chilling cold. "I cannot be harmed by simple shriveling fire spells," said Dazra. Gasping in mock surprise the Lich replied, "My! It seems you must be a special demon." Without bothering to look at his captor Dazra shot back, "I am a half-blood. You can't kill me, cretin!" The Lich took a step back, shocked at this new information, but regained bravado moments later when he said, "Half-blood or pure-blood? Impalement shall hardly brighten your day!" The monstrous magus readied to throw his fiery orb. "Choose your fate or I shall choose for you!" Desperately trying to buy more time, Dazra cried out, "Wait!" as he looked about for a means of escape, "Tell me one thing first!" he said as he tried to loosen his bonds, "How is it that I'm up here imprisoned by you when I clearly remember your defeat against my father?" The Lich chuckled saying, "Even one as mighty as you could not withstand a blow from Ignaros! You were knocked unconscious before you hit the ground" The Lich grimaced and then bellowed, "Now die!" He cut the chain and simultaneously launched the shriveling fire at the dark spikes below. Dazra fell.

Spiraling down toward the ground and the obsidian spikes, Dazra's only thought was, "This isn't going to end well!" Then he thrust his arm out impulsively and cried out, "Veros Islangr parfor Ignaros!" (Come to me, Hammer of Fire!) To his surprise, he heard a mighty explosion.

High above the black spires, the Lich had teleported and retired to his chamber after having dealt with the annoying trespasser and casting the shriveling fire ball to extinguish the pest. Lich was admiring his prize, the war hammer Ignaros, "My beloved hammer," he murmured, chuckling as he stroked the burnished surface. Suddenly, a violent quaking shook the Lich's chamber. "What is this?" exclaimed the sorcerer, as his possessions fell from the shelves around him. He screamed in frustration when the hammer he was holding flew into the earth, plowing at reckless speed towards the main chamber and carrying him along behind.

HIS EYES SHOT UP AS HE REMEMBERED THE BALL OF SHRIVELING FIRE.

Dazra corkscrewed to avoid assorted falling debris. The ground was rushing up to meet him, and he closed his eyes in acceptance of his fate. All of a sudden he gasped. Ignaros had appeared in his right hand! However, still clinging to the hammer was the Lich, who had not consented to this insane trip. Dazra kicked the Lich who released his grip from the hammer. At the same time Dazra glanced down at the spikes and raised the war hammer. Letting loose a primal cry, he collided into the spikes with a mighty crash. The rocks tumbled about, and a huge crater formed in the center. Dazra pulled himself up and looked across at the crippled figure of the Lich who lay semiconscious from the fall. Then his eyes shot up as he remembered the ball of shriveling fire the Lich had cast earlier which was now hurtling down towards them. He mustered what energy he had left and leapt into an empty hollow to his side. Falling hard and rolling, he couldn't help but gaze at the hammer, glowing in his hand, emblazoned with a wolf. A numbing darkness enveloped Verin and all he could hear was a tortured cry echoing from the Lich.

The Reunion

Verin shook himself; he had spent enough time rehashing his painful past. Not to mention surviving the challenging events of the past few days. What with the prison escape, the assassination attempt, being buried alive and an uncomfortable encounter with his older brother, he was ready for a break. He sought refuge in the forgiving forests of Aetheria. As he quietly continued deeper into the trees he was surprised to see a small dwelling up ahead. Verin crouched under the boughs of an oak tree, gazing at the log cabin. "No, it couldn't be?" he murmured. Then, Verin gasped, as he watched a gray robed figure walking through the garden. Suddenly, a deep voice called out, "You know Verin, I might be old, but can still sense that powerful aura you radiate!" The robed figure stopped walking and gazed at the tree, behind which the astonished half-demon crouched. "You needn't try to lure me into the open, I can sense your intentions!" Verin called out. The old man replied, "Even one as crippled as I am can see who is hiding beneath that old beggar disguise!" Over by the cabin, the hooded figure grinned, "True," he uttered, "A beggar might not know of the...delicate condition that plagues you." Verin stood up, and ran to the cabin. "Uncle!" he said, tears filling his eyes, "I've missed you." "I have also missed you," Bruinen said, breaking from Verin's embrace as the two old friends walked into the old wizard's cottage. As if no time had passed their conversation began to flow easily as Verin clutched the steaming cup in his hands, shivering. Bruinen looked up, apparently shaken from his train of thought. "So tell me nephew, how go things in the nether realm?" Verin gazed at his uncle, wearing a quizzical expression. "Erm, it's very, uh, hot..." Bruinen nodded, muttering about his brews and their various effects. "Um, uncle?" Verin asked, looking confused. Bruinen appeared visibly disoriented, shook himself and then as if taking in his surroundings, he slowly relaxed. "I'm terribly sorry, Verin," he said, frowning. "It seems that I, have succumbed to the weariness that accompanies old age." He rubbed his temples pensively. "Please, tell me of your plight." Verin leaned back and sighed. "It appears, uncle, that our fears may soon be realized. We must take action." Bruinen raised an eyebrow, and sat up. "What exactly do you suggest we do?" Verin put down his cup, smoothed his cloak, and began to talk.

"Uncle, as you know my father's ambition is unending. He wishes to control everything in the universe. He thinks himself mightier than the bonds that hold this world together, I have always worried that given enough time, he would attempt to overthrow the natural order of things." Verin paused, and when Bruinen did not respond, continued, "My father is growing old and I feel his energy fields are weakening. My brother Alwyck on the other hand is equally ambitious and thinks this would be an ideal opportunity for him to usurp our father's realm and power." Bruinen scowled, "What harm could come from that? Zarym Malic was ever a fool, always wearing the most cliche of disguises!" Verin, looking even more serious, lowered his voice as if he was afraid to say the words aloud. "My brother, Alwyck seeks to unite the Netherworld and Earth plane. He believes that with those realms conquered, he would be able to delve deeper into other dimensions, and perhaps obtain Godhood!" Bruinen grunted, his brows furrowed, "Child, you told me of this fear many years ago, and we both agreed your brother was delusional!" Verin nodded, but sighed, peering out at the forest, as distant trees waved in the evening breeze. "It seems," Verin spoke quietly, "that Alwyck has enlisted the aid of a human." Bruinen started, his eyes wide. "How?" Verin smiled slightly, gazing with unseeing eyes. "Uncle, it seems that the human in question was called George Carpel, a simple fishmonger from the town of Brine Cove who suddenly disappeared from town. Several weeks passed, and then much to the villagers' surprise someone new arrived in Brine Cove, an individual calling himself Svatan Luciferous. Unbeknownst to the community, the mysterious new member dug up two corpses which he used to perform rituals in the forest. There were rumours of a wraith being seen near Brine Cove. Obvious to the underworld court elders was that the identity of the wraith was indeed, my wayward sibling Alwyck. Further investigation uncovered news that George Carpel's house had been ransacked, and that his portrait had been torn and smeared. Indeed, my brother's plan to use the humans to take power over this land has begun." Verin tore his gaze from the window, stood up, and strolled to the kitchen. "Care for a cup of tea?"

Bruinen rose from his chair, leaning on his staff. "What do you suggest we do to stop this?" Verin returned, holding two cups of tea. "I simply need to find the most powerful weapon that exists in the known universe." chuckled Verin, knowing full well the gravity of the task.

"Right, well I'd best be off!" grinned Verin as he shouldered his pack. "Farewell, Uncle." Bruinen smiled, leaning on the doorframe, "Good hunting, to you and your cousins!" Verin managed to grin even wider, and ran into the forest, toward Brine Cove.

Several days had passed since Verin's visit. After spending the morning working in his herb garden sorting out specific plants for drying, Bruinen decided it was time to head inside and attend to some unfinished business. "Let's see what that thief was able to extract from my atlas," Bruinen said to himself, closing the door. He began leafing through what remained of the Accursed Atlas, and something caught his eye. He peered closer, and gently scratched the binding which to his surprise, began to flake. He pressed harder and an entire section of the book peeled off. "Blast!" he had been tricked by a simple bait and switch tactic. Which meant that the real Accursed Atlas had fallen into the wrong hands. His thoughts raced in all directions trying to calculate the damage that could be unleashed. Bruinen's face paled, incredibly alarmed by this new turn of events. He uncovered the front of the ancient book. There he found a message inscribed on the tome which was even more ominous: "You have lost more than you think." The signature was messy and blurred, but it was clearly written in bluish-green blood. Bruinen rushed to the door, but instinct held him back. "This isn't right, there's something wrong!" he thought just as a whistling sound alerted him to the wave of arrows speeding towards him.

As the threat of the arrows bore down upon him, Bruinen fondly remembered a special afternoon he had spent laughing with his nephew, which had quickly turned from sorrow to joy. "I'm telling you Uncle! Something is coming and Ezekiel will be called upon to meet the challenge!" Bruinen cursed himself for letting Verin know about Ezekiel's existence so early. "He's only a boy! You can't put that kind of pressure on him!" Verin frowned, "He took on Nos Nethrakos Lycan! Are you trying to tell me he can't handle pressure? He needs to be ready to fight!" It was Bruinen's turn to frown, "What I'm trying to say is that you seem to forget he is only a child! Seven years to manhood. You, of all people should know what can happen in the span of seven years!" Verin shrank slightly, "Yes, I know, but I still think he should be prepared, for anything he might come up against, not the least of which is my father."

Then, almost imperceptibly, Bruinen heard a slight sob and felt pity on Verin, knowing that the loss of a parent, even one so despicable as Hell's Shadow, could take its toll. "Mmm, well I suppose a little magic never hurt anyone, Bruinen chuckled with a glint in his eye. Verin looked up and began to laugh as well. Soon, a rousing chorus of laughter could be heard. Why was it that memories of times when he enjoyed the feeling of being alive came so easily at this late stage in his life? He was grateful for the comfort that the recollection had provided considering the dire situation he was now facing.

One solitary arrow pierced Bruinen's chest.

The Downfall

Swiftly, Bruinen began to utter an ancient spell, but this was not an incantation of attack or defense. Rather, it was a song, describing all that he had lived, loved, and hated and it represented the fullest expression of himself. The hordes of hellish demons that had begun their charging attack, had no idea what they were about to face. Suddenly, points of brilliant light shot toward the clearing from every direction. Each light carried within it a virtuous mage, wizard, or witch from within a hundred leagues. All had raced to Bruinen's aid once they had received the old potion master's cry for help, known to them as the "Finarik Mortuos" (a final lamentation).

A company of demons the size and likes of which had not been seen since the Hundred Years War were poised to wreak havoc upon Bruinen's cottage. However, in the same instant all the virtuous servants combined their mystical strength to neutralize the airborne attack. Unfortunately however, one solitary arrow passed through their shield and pierced Bruinen Bright-Talon's chest, very close to his heart. Yet, in the same moment, Bruinen felt himself being summoned by magic. He staggered into the living room, grasped his staff, threw on his cloak, and barely had time to pick up the vial of wraith's blood before he was whisked away into a maelstrom of energy. Meanwhile, back at Bruinen's cottage the combined magi of Aetheria managed to vapourize every last demon, save those who had chosen to run. However, in the aftermath of battle, once his cottage had been thoroughly searched, no one could find the desperate potion master.

Tereleth was rudely awoken by a vicious kick to her side. She sat up, coughing. "Get up quickly or we'll stab ya and leave ya to bleed out, we've been discovered!" a voice whispered. The sky was still dark, but in the distance the queen could hear men's voices, accompanied by horses' hooves and clanking of armour. The band of thieves quickly and efficiently gathered their possessions, rolled up their beds, and in the span of five minutes, they were all mounted and racing for the south. Tereleth's gag had been removed while she slept, and so she took a calculated risk in shouting out. "Help, I've been kidnapped! Help!" The thieves rode harder, evading their pursuers but a well-aimed arrow sank into the thigh of the mule that Tereleth was riding with a thunk! and she tumbled to the ground. After a few minutes, the armed guard who had chased the bandits arrived accompanied by none other than Othmar. "Milady, I knew you wanted to find Ezekiel, but you really ought to have given me a bit more warning!" Her manservant smiled, as he helped her to her feet. Tereleth embraced the meek man and thanked him. "They took my ring, the one Ezekiel gave me." Othmar nodded, "Do not worry, Your Majesty." He stepped away from the queen to address his troop, gesturing to the men, "Onward men, and find those dogs!" A spark of passion coloured his voice, spurring them to find the band of thieves who had wronged their queen. Othmar turned to Tereleth, "On the matter of Ezekiel, I believe I know where we can find him." Tereleth hesitated as she recalled Bruinen's warning, but then she felt a tiny flutter inside her womb. She touched a hand to her stomach, and feeling her baby's presence she straightened her back and with a resolute expression replied, "No, I must find my husband, for better or worse, he needs me, and we need him." Othmar nodded, leading two horses into view, "We've been tracking those bandits for several days now, and we think they may know where Ezekiel is. Or at least who captured Kalleth." Tereleth raised an eyebrow, "How on earth could you possibly know?" Othmar smiled, "Because we have a man on the inside, a thief who isn't as unscrupulous as the rest." Tereleth shook her head in amazement, and as she mounted the horse she gasped. "What is it, Your Majesty?" Othmar rushed over, concerned. Tereleth barely concealed a groan, "They have returned, I am experiencing a desperate craving for cabbage." Othmar reached inside the saddlebag and pulled out a full head of cabbage. "I anticipated your cravings, Your Highness, and brought with me as large a variety of food as I could carry." Tereleth felt touched, saying, "You are too kind." The manservant scratched his head, "Lucius will probably be disappointed that his secret stash of vegetables has been raided." Tereleth smiled at the thought of the intimidating knight rummaging through his saddlebag, unable to find his cabbage. And so it was they rode on, in search of the bandits who had stolen Tereleth's ring and her brother-in-law.

Tereleth and Othmar caught up with their troop only to find themselves in yet another sticky situation. The king's guard had been ambushed by the very bandits they had been tracking. Now, the unsavoury group was aiming bows and swords at them with unflinching steadiness. The leader of the group stepped forward, a man who Tereleth remembered with unrelenting enmity. He entered the centre of the circle, and she could finally see him clearly. She grudgingly admitted that he was handsome, having a long mane of well groomed raven black hair and emerald-green eyes like gems. His left cheek was bandaged, and she smiled inwardly, for she had inflicted the wound in one of her attempts to escape. "Well, it appears we have quite an odd little pack of wolves, trailing us even as we try to evade them." The leader smiled, "My name is Verin. Verin Elhadhir." He turned to his allies, flashing a toothy smile, "Now boys, lay down your weapons, and let me show you how to put down wolves!" The thieves complied, some of them mumbling about how he was ruthless and didn't need their help. Verin turned and faced Othmar. Tereleth noticed as an unspoken recognition passed between them. The leader of the bandits grabbed his mane of well combed black locks, and promptly removed it from his head with a flourish. Underneath were his natural locks of cropped brown hair, which she admitted, looked more fitting. Yet even more impressive, he kept his back turned to the shocked bandits, as he projected a fireball behind him, causing the band to scatter. "Best be off lads!" he yelled over his shoulder, "That particular spell is rather incendiary!" He walked over to the horsemen as the fiery sphere exploded behind him. "A pleasure to finally meet you, Your Royal Highness," he said as he dropped into an elegant bow before her. "Verin Elhadhir, cousin to Ezekiel and Kalleth, and devoted servant of the realm."

The Thief No More

The Royal Guard set up camp in a clearing near the thieves' old hideout, and once comfortably settled Verin entertained them with an impressive tale. "You see, Your Majesty, Ezekiel had been too young to remember me as the generous nobleman who had come to their rescue so long ago. Kalleth had no way of knowing I was his blood relation, and so Bruinen and I agreed 'twas in their best interest that he should care for them as they grew. I have kept watch over them from a distance and as such was alarmed to learn of Kalleth's disappearance. I have been traveling for quite a few days with these ruffians, tracking Ezekiel's progress as we went. The previous leader of the band was a truly unpleasant fellow, but having lived with them, I believe that some of them possess a spark of goodness within them. It seems that your husband is making for Brine Cove, and so that's where we must be go, but I need to warn you, dark forces have come into play, and none of us shall come away unchanged." Tereleth nodded, "That reminds me Othmar," she turned to her servant. "How did you manage to keep the realm from crumbling with both rulers absent from the throne?" Othmar chuckled, coming out of his shell more and more as Tereleth got to know him. "Your Majesty, that was a simple matter of arranging a peculiar schedule which included no public appearances. A great deal of gold changed hands I'll admit, but you may rest easy knowing that the kingdom is convinced that you are bedridden upon doctor's orders to ensure the safety of the realm's future heir to the throne and that you desire no audience of any kind." Tereleth sighed, and sat back on the log which was positioned closely to the fire. "And you," she addressed Verin. "What of those magical skills you demonstrated earlier? That was an impressive display of power if I ever saw one." Verin's eyes grew more serious, "Believe me Your Majesty when I tell you that the subject of my past is one I won't discuss." Tereleth prodded further, "I said nothing about your past. What are you hiding? You claim to serve the realm." Verin got up, "Your Majesty, I serve the Crown, but it has been a relatively recent pledge and I am quite sure that discussing my past shall not prevent any assassinations and might in fact provoke one. Good night, Tereleth." He nodded to Othmar and entered his tent, leaving his use of the queen's name hanging in the air.

Tereleth sat silent for a time, pondering their new ally's words. "Othmar, how do you know each other?" The servant replied hesitantly at first, but then words flooded from him like a river. "I have been a servant of the crown for thirty years, for your father, and his father before him. A while ago, perhaps a month before he was killed, he sent me and several of his royal guard to a secluded clearing on the other end of Autrum Lake. There in the clearing was a small hill with a cave, concealed by fallen branches and rocks yes, but visible all the same. We followed a tunnel within the cave until we reached a lair of sorts. The space was neat and tidy, but you wouldn't believe the amount of treasure chests we found there, all them were neatly sorted from left to right; precious gems, gold coins, ancient artifacts and one particular chest which we could not open was adorned with runes of various kinds and possessed a dragon's head shaped lock. We had hauled all of the treasure from the cave and were loading our carts when Verin arrived. The man was incredible, dispatching two thirds of our men within seconds when the rest surrendered. Then the guard shocked me, for no sooner had Verin turned his back, than they knocked him out cold and placed him in shackles." Othmar's face grew more expressive as he continued on, "Before the day was out, we had logged another prisoner into Gloomwick's jail and significantly bolstered the royal treasury. However, the strangest thing about the mission was to follow; before the prisoner was knocked unconscious by the guard, he spoke with me. Verin asked me what I thought about the treasure and what my life was like, and he didn't seem to be a criminal in the slightest, despite the fact that the lair was obviously his. His curiosity and desire to learn surprised me. However, when the day was done, I didn't give the mysterious Verin Elhadhir another thought. On a more recent mission with the guard we went to the cabin in the woods, and encountered Bruinen and 'Silver Tooth' as Verin was once called. None of the guard from the first encounter attended on this mission, and as such Bruinen explained Verin's relation to you and Ezekiel. The wizard warned me not to tell you about their blood tie unless Verin himself was to speak of it. Your new uncle Bruinen is a funny man for he enjoys the gathering of secrets, but is quite stingy in the sharing of them. In any case, after having had two opportunities to meet the man, I recognized him immediately once we arrived to rescue you.

"I'm still mystified by how quickly he won over that group of bandits. I cannot believe that here we are, a queen searching for her king, a manservant who is more resourceful than he seems and a criminal with a lust for gold turned hero. Let us soon find the king!" And with that, Othmar yawned and went into his tent, leaving Tereleth only semi-satisfied as she still had many questions swimming through her head.

The next morning after a traveler's breakfast of nuts, dried meat, and fruit, the horses and bags were quickly packed for departure. Verin motioned to Tereleth to ride closer. "Your Majesty, I would advise you to stay back with Othmar in case something goes wrong." Tereleth frowned, "You say that like you expect something to go wrong." Verin nodded, "It's a strong possibility, and even if nothing does, I'd like to be the first to speak to Ezekiel, as there is a matter of great importance that Bruinen desired I tell him as soon as possible." Tereleth grumbled, but agreed, noting that somehow the bright-eyed and handsome cousin always got his way.

Verin stood at the edge of the forest just outside of Brine Cove. He gazed at the horizon, deep in contemplation of his past, as a new conviction settled into his mind. "No matter what evils I have committed in the past in service to my father and the Netherworld, the actions I choose in the coming days will no doubt determine who I truly am, and how I will be remembered!" The wind ruffled his hair gently. He sat up straighter when he spied the object for which he had been patiently waiting. "It's about time you showed up cousin," he muttered, gazing down upon Brine Cove. He watched as Ezekiel rode through the small village on his jet black steed. Verin slowly grinned sensing the pulse of magic as he strode down the hills toward the village watching as Ezekiel dismounted and ran over to the boathouse. Verin was eager to meet his Bright-Talon cousin. However, he knew the queen and the royal guard were just behind him atop the hill so that he didn't have much time to pass on Bruinen's message.

As Verin reached the town square, a shadow fell over him. "Hello, half-brother." He turned to see the familiar figure of Alwyck, and his hand went defensively to his sword. "What are you doing here?" Verin asked, startled. "I'm in the process of finding the Staff of Seasons for Father!" Alwyck smirked, "I don't believe you, halfling." In a condescending tone Alwyck carried on, "My dear brother, I know you never planned to help father do his dirty work, and you should know that the Netherworld has had a change in management." In a surprising move Alwyck struck his brother much as a viper attacks without warning. He punched Verin with such force that he crashed through the walls of an old stable, debris tumbling down around him. Verin looked up at his brother in shock, then his brow set in determination; this cowardly usurper would not get away with his devious plan. Verin jumped up, blade at the ready, Alwyck chuckled and waved a hand, causing the remains of the stable to crash down on top of Verin. Alwyck turned away, straightening his turban. "That'll keep you busy." He muttered, as he turned to leave. Beneath the layers of rubble, Verin could still sense his brother's intent, and struggled fruitlessly against the dusty prison. "Damn."

Tereleth watched the scene unfold in shock, "Othmar, we need to help Verin!" Tears ran down her cheeks as she watched the building fall on top of her new friend. Othmar simply held her in his lanky arms, and grimly brought them to a clearing several paces away. "Tereleth, that wizard just brought down a building. The only logical course of action is to escape to safety." Tereleth couldn't see as tears blurred her vision. "We've got to help him. Nobody else will!" Othmar cringed, "I know, but the best way we can help would be to elude the clutches of that monster." He looked at her stomach. "Wouldn't Ezekiel want us to safeguard his beautiful wife and heir? Your pregnancy has always been at risk, and now I fear the stress could be too much." Tereleth sat in the grass and sobbed. She couldn't convince Othmar to help rescue Verin. Suddenly, one of the guards yelled out a warning, just as an explosion silenced him. A darkly robed figure walked calmly through the crowd, besting horseman after horseman. Othmar leapt in front of the queen and the ominous figure stopped. "Ah, such a tragedy you are. Poor Othmar. I can read your mind. I know the secrets that you keep! I can see that the queen has always held a special place in your heart. You desired to take her for a wife and yet she fell in love with another and oops! The shining knight wins again!" The man's grin was a veil that he often used to disguise his true intentions almost as effectively as the turban he wore wrapped around his head hid his hair. Othmar gasped, looking back at Tereleth, who had never known of his secret admiration for her. "I am so sorry I couldn't protect you, my queen," he managed to say, just as his chest was run through by an already bloody blade.

The turbaned menace crossed closer to the queen. Tereleth could only back away slowly, as she tripped over the body of a fallen guard. "Good day, Your Majesty. It is indeed an honour to finally meet you! I'm afraid your brave protector has failed you; he was something of a wimp. In any case, I'd love to know why I can sense another life is present here, when you and I are the last ones standing? Methinks you look kind of bloated around the belly. Best to wear black dear, it's very slimming." With a flourish, he shot a band of black ropes around her. Tereleth was so completely enwrapped that only a small hole remained near her nose and mouth. Kneeling beside the now prone queen, Alwyck whispered into her ear. "Darling, you and your pup will make a great addition to my trophy room."

Chronicle Four: The Gift of the Gods

The Horde

The smells of smoke, fire, blood, and sulfur assaulted Kalleth's nose. He smelled destruction, saw chaos, and heard the very churnings of hell itself. In the back of his mind he could sense the sting of his wounds. He was most aware of the environment around him. "What happened?" he thought, "How did everything go so wrong?" They had been winning the battle, but the tides had turned dramatically when Svatan used his magic to reanimate every soldier they had cut down, thus creating an unending enemy to defeat. "It's not fair!" he thought desperately as he witnessed a maelstrom of demonic power and destruction. He became vaguely aware of a thundering sound, which was growing louder. Kalleth tried to ignore the ominous sound. "What we need," he thought caustically, "is a demonic counterpart, someone of their kind to turn the tide in our favour!" He dismissed the thought as wishful thinking. Suddenly, he was roused from his stupor by the victory cries made by hordes of new demons who crawled through the fissure in the courtyard. For a brief moment Kalleth could see Ezekiel lying on the ground several feet in front of him. In the next instant they were both captured and scooped up by the wave of demons. It took Kalleth several seconds before he realized they were heading into a massive crevasse in the courtyard. "Kalleth!" yelled Ezekiel. Kalleth wrenched around in an attempt to locate his brother. Despite a great deal of thrashing in an attempt to escape his captors, the hole loomed ever closer. Dreading what would happen next, he searched for his weapons, alas they had been confiscated. In the blink of a mortal eye, the entire company was swallowed up into the earth, and the fissure closed. All was suddenly quiet.

———•◆•———

The last thing Ezekiel remembered was the whole world going inky black, as if the sun itself had been snuffed out. Suddenly, the temperature became ice cold, and yet his skin burned with the heat of one hundred fires. However, once his eyes began to adjust he could just make out strange colours and patterns. Ezekiel gasped as all of a sudden the grunting, squealing, and general ruckus created by the hoarde of demons was translated into a language he could understand inside his head. Chills ran up his spine when beneath him, he overheard the conversation between his two demonic captors, "Oy, watch your tail you dirty rotten-" A loud *thud* erupted. "You watch your tail, Rauros! Keep your voice down or we'll both be thrashed!" The other voice replied. "Jeez, alrigh' I'll calm down! No need to go blabbering on!" A *clink* sounded and Ezekiel felt a forceful jab in his thigh. "Whaddya think the boss wants us to do with fatty here?" Ezekiel resisted the urge to voice his objection, "Beats me, he ain't much good 'cept for cooking up as a midday snack!" Ezekiel reached for his weapon but was disappointed to find it was missing.

———•◆•———

Bruinen was shocked when the transportation spell deposited him next to Kalleth, who was being held captive in a deep trance. In the moments that followed Bruinen spied Ezekiel who seemed to be engaged in a shouting match with the two demons carrying him. A massive hoard of demons was trudging through an inter-dimensional tunnel that stretched between the boundaries of time and space. Upon his apparition Bruinen had been quickly captured and with his energy flagging he turned his attention to the demons carrying him. From their garbled and curse-riddled speech, he understood that Alwyck had commanded that the prisoners be brought to his Netherworld stronghold. An aching pain radiated from the arrow wound he had sustained, but Bruinen was not able to heal himself. With hundreds of devilish fiends surrounding them, Bruinen could only pray that Bright-Talon loyalties spanned the dimensions.

———•◆•———

Ezekiel knew trouble was brewing when he saw the obsidian fortress looming ahead. His lungs burned from the scorching air which grew that much heavier and hotter due to the lava pooling beneath the path. He had long since given up trying to make his two demons captors shut up, so he was surprised when all at once the assembly grew quiet. Suddenly, Ezekiel heard Kalleth cry out, as he saw several demons fall into the glowing river. The snarling voice of Zarym Malic boomed through the ranks, "Where is the seer?" Ezekiel's eyes widened and his gut twisted when his eyes caught sight of the minotaur from his nightmares. He froze temporarily as his mind flashed back to the battle he had fought as a boy. Ezekiel watched dumbfounded as the surly beast snatched up his brother. Kalleth cursed aloud and thrust his hand forward crying out, "Thrysta Glacia!" (Throw Ice!) However, nothing happened. The entire assembly of demons broke into cruel, mocking laughter. "Magic is our blood, and this is our realm. You are bold to attempt magic in my presence," Zarym Malic proclaimed. Kalleth sneered, "It seems I must resort to more ancient methods." Zarym Malic frowned, "What are you talking about?" *Bam!* Quick as lightning, Kalleth struck the minotaur's snout with his fist. "AARGH!" Clutching at his nose the angry beast released Kalleth. Leaping over the bull-man's shoulder and grasping one of Zarym's horns, Kalleth cried out, "Krakvaros!" (Victory!) With a strength rarely shown, Kalleth snapped the minotaur's horn clean off.

Kalleth snapped the minotaur's horn clean off.

Kalleth had known his escape attempt was pointless, but causing pain and chaos provided some small satisfaction, as did hearing the minotaur scream from the wounds he had inflicted. He was held captive in a poorly lit cell, which smelled of things best left undisturbed. He had grown accustomed to the ever present waves of heat, which left him drenched in sweat. He was also adapting to the rusty aftertaste in the water they had given him, which was the only thing keeping him from dying of dehydration. Kalleth could not shake the feeling that all hope was lost. Here he was, again locked away to be forgotten. He recalled how the purple-robed lady had helped him once before, so he began to meditate, a skill which helped to calm his nerves in the heat of battle, aided in his ability to see through the deception of others, and assisted him when he was using magic. It was almost second nature to him. He desperately hoped that he would be able to contact the mysterious woman. Deep in concentration, he focused as several minutes passed. "You called?" Kalleth nearly choked when the feminine voice echoed in his mind. "Um, hello?" he hesitated. No answer. He tried again to contact her but used his thoughts instead of his voice. "It took you long enough," the same echoing voice replied. "Who are you?" Kalleth thought, frightened that the voice was a trick of his mind. A beautiful laugh that gave him chills sounded, "I assure you I am real. Do not worry, help is coming. Be brave." Just like that, the presence vanished from Kalleth's mind, leaving him with more questions than answers.

Bruinen could not help feeling that he was living the good life. At first, he had been intimidated by the mounted heads and multicolored torches, but now they seemed quite familiar almost comforting. He didn't care that his butler had too many heads to count, and why should he? The food was divine and the ice water was cool but not chilling. He saw no reason to do anything but enjoy his surroundings. Yet in the back of his mind, there seemed to be something he desperately needed to do. Something incredibly urgent. Somehow, he knew the bandage on his shoulder had something to do with it. "Milord, thy roast lamb!" said the butler, looking in all directions at once.

Excellent! thought Bruinen, and the wisp of memory containing his nephews and their perilous predicament slipped quite literally from his mind.

The Reluctant Return

Escaping the rubble his brother had trapped him under had taken some time but Verin had been up to the task. Though his liberation had taken the better part of a day and a half to accomplish he was ready to battle against Alwyck. As a new dawn brightened the horizon, Verin had carefully crossed over to the island that housed his brother's fortress and reviewed his options. "I could go straight into the nether realm and try to find Ezekiel and Kalleth, but maybe there is another way..." he murmured to himself. Below him lay the shadowy courtyard where the battle had raged. He had only just arrived in time to see the enormous rift in the ground closing. Even more disturbingly, after searching the courtyard for signs of any life or for clues, he had found a ring. A strange artifact indeed, the ring was eerily fashioned to appear as though the sun was peeking through the clouds. So mysterious was the ring that when Verin first spied it, he wondered if the circle might hold magic. Upon further inspection, it appeared to be plainly made of iron with gold trim. However, distracted as Verin was by his predicament he stuffed the ring into his pocket. The first beams of light penetrated the murk of the courtyard. "Well, let's see if I can call up the incantation..." Verin grinned and then ran hurriedly into a dark corner. When the sun finally touched this point, Verin was long gone.

———•◆•———

That all things in life were not equal was quickly becoming apparent to Verin. Crossing between realms continued to be exceedingly tedious, and his bad mood did not improve once he arrived at his father's demonic palace. The place brought back bad memories, which gave Verin a chill down his spine. He crept along the blackened corridors, searching for the dungeon. At one point during his search, he heard a guard, rushing through the hall. Ducking into an alcove, Verin watched silently as the goblin scurried past. Relieved, he sank to the floor, breathing heavily from anxiety and exhaustion. He was trying to catch his breath, when unexpectedly the wall behind him began to buzz. Jumping up, Verin regarded the wall uneasily. Suddenly, the floor beneath him fell away, and he dropped. Panicking, Verin attempted to break his fall, by grasping at the walls. Looking up, he saw the hole through which he had fallen seal shut. For several minutes, he fell at great speed, wondering if the passage even had an end. Gradually, the tunnel began to level off, finally Verin was launched from the chute into an underground chamber. The air smelled heavily of incense and the room was smoldering hot. A roar broke the silence, deafening in its proximity. Then right away, he saw the hammer. On a bronze pedestal, Ignaros, the flaming hammer, was propped up. Twin beams of light illuminated the mythical weapon. Despite the bloodcurdling cry, Verin strode toward Ignaros. Before he could reach his goal, a wall of force launched him through the air. Landing heavily on the ground, Verin looked up, vision blurring. "You took forever!" a female voice screeched, "Your uncle and cousins are imprisoned and possibly dying!" Verin, who'd been dizzy before, now had to contend with ringing in his ears. Due to these distractions, he paid little attention to the woman standing before him. He attempted to silence her by swiping at her leg meekly, and his hand passed straight through. "Who are you?" Verin groaned, pushing a hand under himself. Once again, he was knocked over by the piercing scream that echoed through the room. "You are the most selfish person I know! Leaving your family to die? For what? Some shiny hammer?" Verin rested on his knees, and raised an eyebrow. "That 'shiny hammer' could mean the difference between beating Alwyck and our destruction!" Standing up fully, Verin glared at her, "I'd say that you were the person meddling here." The lady, wearing a violet robe, turned a similar shade of purple, whether in anger or due to embarrassment. "Just take your stupid hammer, and go rescue them!" Verin regarded her with a puzzled expression, "That was always my goal, why do you find it so important to question my integrity?" The purple robed lady turned to walk away, "I just hope you know where your loyalties lie..." She tossed an object into a corner, and vanished.

 Verin walked over to the object and gasped, eyes widening. Lying on the chamber floor was a charred piece of rock, upon which was carved two words, "Dazra Malic." Confused and scared, Verin rushed to the pedestal, grabbed the hammer, and ran. He raced up a staircase located behind the pedestal and found a dead end. He searched for a catch or lever, and finally he discovered a hidden button. Pressing it, the mechanism activated and opened into a prison cell.

TWIN BEAMS OF LIGHT ILLUMINATED THE MYTHICAL WEAPON.

Kalleth was starting to think the world had forgotten about him when suddenly the the walls started shaking. He hadn't managed to locate any entrance to the cell beforehand, so he was astonished when all at once one of the walls vanished. He received an even greater surprise when he saw the figure who stood in front of him. A slim but muscled man strode into the cell, carrying an intimidating hammer. Kalleth attempted to stand, but was restricted by his chains. "Who are you?" The mysterious figure walked slowly towards him, and raised his massive mace. With one mighty swing, he shattered the bonds holding Kalleth prisoner. "Follow me," he said, cryptically. Kalleth rose, and nearly fell over. The man caught him, and asked, "Are you okay?" Kalleth grunted, shrugging off the other man's grip. "Let's just say it's been a rough day." He glanced at his rescuer, "You still haven't answered my question. Who are you, and why are you helping me to escape?" The man grinned, and dropped to one knee. "Verin Elhadhir, at your service!" He gestured to the door, "We better be going." Kalleth nodded, and started to leave. "Oh, and by the way, it's going to be a bumpy ride," Verin called out. Kalleth, puzzled by this statement, tried to keep pace with his new ally. Verin observed Kalleth with an unsettling interest. Verin asked, "So, what's your name? Forgive me, but I think after that amazing rescue, you owe me a name." Kalleth's expression tightened; he was annoyed by Verin's abrupt conversation. Upon hearing Kalleth's name, all colour drained from Verin's face and he looked as though he'd seen a ghost. "What's wrong?" Kalleth asked, confused. Suddenly, Verin tackled him to the floor, gagged him, and shoved him into a corner in the space of three seconds. Kalleth was unable to express his outrage, but was quickly silenced by the sound of hooves, thundering up the staircase. He watched, as Verin's hammer started to smoke.

———•◆•———

Once he'd safely hidden Kalleth, Verin rose to face his father. As each thundering step grew closer, Verin became increasingly afraid. Verin's hammer began to smoke, which at first had surprised him, but then he closed his eyes and focussed his mind, drawing upon the weapon's magic energy. Several tiny bluish flames licked across the length of Ignaros. Like a shot Zarym Malic burst forth roaring onto the ledge. The angry minotaur regarded the scene blankly, and then realization crossed his face that Verin, his weak son, held Ignaros in his undeserving hand. The wild minotaur charged ferociously towards his prey, his remaining, singular horn gleaming. Verin had not failed to notice that Zarym had been weakened by the loss of his horn among other visible injuries. Verin began to target the injured areas of the Minotaur's body, as he sent a fireball to the snout, a swift blow to the stubby remains of the horn, and landed a vicious kick to the beast's right ankle. Soon, the massive bull-man had been reduced to a whimpering mess, lying prostrate on the floor. An impressive transformation for one who was once so universally feared. Word of this defeat would certainly shatter his fierce reputation. "Where are you holding my friends?" Verin questioned, thrusting his hammer to Zarym's throat. His father's eyes bulged as he spat out, "You have no friends, you freak of both realms, you are a monster, an abomination!" Verin smirked in response to his father's insults. Putting more pressure behind his hammer, Verin ignited the hammer, but with a catch. Deep violet flowed slowly down the flames. "If you have any sense left at all, you will tell me where my friends are imprisoned." All at once the fight seemed to go out of his father's eyes as he conceded his defeat saying, "Th-th-they are at the fifth floor of the lower district. Don't use the shriveling fire, I beg you!" Verin withdrew his hammer. "You must have been extremely angry to have imprisoned them in that infernal hell." He turned away from the father he had once feared above all and muttered a word under his breath and suddenly Kalleth's bonds disappeared. Standing up and rubbing at his wrists Kalleth came out of his hiding spot and said, "You're cocky for a man who just beat someone with a powerful disadvantage." Zarym groaned in protest but was quickly silenced by a glare from Kalleth. "What shall we do with our prisoner?" Verin looked over at the broken beast, and a single tear slid down his cheek. Verin hoped his cousin would mistake the moisture for sweat, he grabbed Kalleth by the shoulder and said, "Leave him. Let's go."

The Past Revealed

Impossible as it seemed, the heat grew even more intense as Kalleth and Verin snuck down into the demonic jail. The first level they explored was littered with massive generators rumbling. Looking carefully, Kalleth could just barely see the labourers struggling to work their machines. "Each level imprisons a different type of offender." Verin whispered, motioning for Kalleth to follow. "This level is for traitors from wealthy backgrounds, individuals who have never had to work for themselves. They are charged with betraying their superiors and as punishment they are condemned to operate these machines." Verin entered the next chamber with a disgusted look on his face. "What the prisoners don't know is that the machines are designed to do absolutely nothing. Their labour is futile." Kalleth grimaced, and followed his companion down the hallway. Glancing from side to side, he noticed various shafts housing all manners of travel. Stairs, which were in dismal repair, had been discarded for more exotic solutions. Ropes and chains shook faintly, likely from the guards using them to move between floors. Other devices whose purpose remained a mystery hung haphazardly on the walls, some with lethal looking spikes. Verin's eyes narrowed, and he sniffed the air, crouching low to the ground. Without any notice the shaft began to shake, the stairs began to crumble and the items on the wall including the spikes retracted into the wall. "Guards! Get down!" yelled Verin, ducking out of the shaft, pulling Kalleth with him. The quaking grew stronger and faster and there was an enormous crash as a platform fell into place, edges steaming and walls crackling. The door slammed open to reveal a cohort of devilish guards. Verin gazed at the scene, dumbfounded. Kalleth elbowed him, "Maybe we ought to draw our weapons?" Verin blinked, "Right." he nodded in agreement as Kalleth drew his rapier. Verin merely grasped his hammer and shrugged. They both jumped into the still-smoking room. A cacophony of chaos issued up the shaft. If any guards had survived they would have said that the chamber was a great deal messier after their encounter.

Inside the strange room, Verin was scanning a desk overflowing with buttons, levers, and switches, not to mention much gore. "Ah, here we are," he said, flipping a lever and turning to face Kalleth. "I've managed to figure out this device. It appears there are a system of pulleys - fueled by the hard labours of yet more prisoners - raising and lowering this chamber." He turned to a separate panel covered in numbered buttons. "This," Verin gestured, "is how the guards communicate which floor they want to reach. Those crystals we saw in the shaft, they send a chain of lights up to the supervisor who then operates the machinery, or rather he inspires the prisoners to pull faster." Kalleth smirked, looking over the blood-spattered panel. "All very fascinating, but how are we going to rescue my uncle and brother?" Verin sighed, and pressed a button very near the bottom. "That's not so easily explained, we entered the shaft at the Upper District, level seven hundred. Bruinen and Ezekiel are supposed to be on the fifth level of the Lower District, which means we are going-" Suddenly, Kalleth pinned Verin up against the wall, shock dawning on his face, rapier to Verin's throat. "How do you know their names? Who are you? For that matter, why did you rescue me?" Verin looked up at him, eyes shining. "I had hoped we could work together without you ever finding out. However, by all appearances I've failed." Kalleth frowned, "What are you talking about? Why should I trust you? How do I know you aren't taking me to be captured and tortured" Verin flicked the blade away, and sheathed his hammer. "Because I love you."

Verin closed his eyes and pictured his life of twenty years ago. He began to speak, slowly at first, but then more comfortably as he grew into the rhythm. "At the tender age of six, you and Ezekiel were abandoned in the wilderness by your alcoholic father. During that time Bruinen Bright-Talon was still very active in routing out demons and did not know of his brother's homeless children. Kalleth, you spent most of your time scavenging for food. Both of you barely survived the hardships you endured. On one particularly severe night, the rain was pouring down relentlessly, and everything was drenched. You were lying unconscious under a tree, and both you and Ezekiel were dying from the extreme exposure and starvation. Not far down the road a kindhearted nobleman was sheltering under the eaves of the tavern. After retrieving his horse from the stable boy, the man headed for home. However his trip was cut short by the cry of a child. He investigated and found, much to his surprise, two small children huddled under a maple tree in the forest clearing. He was dismayed to see the spectre of death hovering near. Hurriedly, the man picked them up and rode swiftly to a cabin in the woods.

The next morning, you and Ezekiel awoke to find a steaming breakfast and warm cups of milk. For months afterward, you were kept safe and your bellies full by an unseen benefactor. Then, one day while you were exploring the market, your uncle Bruinen saw you and Ezekiel playing among the stalls and he recognized his brother's features on your faces. Bruinen followed you to the cabin in the woods which also happened to belong to Bruinen. In that moment Bruinen understood who had brought you to shelter there and the reasons why I kept my distance. I was the one watching over you all this time, aiding you whenever help was required. Bruinen and I have been working against my father's forces for years. Zarym Malic, the brutish minotaur you just relieved of a horn, fell in love with your aunt, who bore him a child. She was my mother and that devil, my father. I am your cousin, and hopefully now your friend, Verin Bright-Talon.

Verin finished his tale, and cleared his throat, "We should get going then." Kalleth sheathed his weapon. "I just have one question." Verin turned, "Yes?" Kalleth gripped the wall, as the chamber shook in its descent. "Are you a demon?" Verin began to shudder, a chill ran down his spine. *Oh no.* He had forgotten about the dramatic effect remaining in the nether realm would have on his human body. Verin gasped, "Not entirely, but it now occurs to me that you might want to stand back." He fell to his knees, shaking and coughing.

Kalleth stepped back as Verin shook and hacked. Spikes protruded from his spine, fangs sprouted in his mouth. His skin rippled and tore into scales. Claws grew, and Verin's back arched painfully. His eyes burst open, his pupils turned angular, and the whites of his eyes glazed over blood-red. A guttural growl rose from within. Suddenly, he roared viciously. Kalleth cried out, "Verin? What's wrong?" The reptilian Verin stood up and stumbled. "Ugh, this isn't good," he muttered, leaning on the wall. "Bruinen warned me about this, I'm returning to my corporeal form." Kalleth hesitantly poked his friend's arm, "Um, corporeal? This seems solid." Verin fidgeted, "Quit it! Any demonic being, even a half demon, like me, wears a different form in each realm. The nether realm has begun to take predominance. This is my corporeal form." Kalleth, who had withdrawn his hand quickly, looked visibly shaken and turned to watch the panel of numbers. Shifting uncomfortably, he said, "Well, it appears that we have some time before we reach level five."

SPIKES PROTRUDED FROM VERIN'S SPINE, AND FANGS SPROUTED IN HIS MOUTH.

The Memories Return

Bruinen felt very cold. He had no idea how much time had passed since he had been captured. Only moments before, he had woken up in his cell bruised and tired. He recalled being tortured by an illusion of decadence. Fortunately, he began to notice inconsistencies in the facade and the whole hallucination collapsed. He scanned his prison cell and noted that his breath was crystallizing in the air. Being no fool, Bruinen knew that if he wasn't rescued soon, he would die. A simple flame spell should suffice he mused and reaching into the depths of his mind, he tried to recall the words of power. *What? I know this spell but now, it's...gone! How can this be?* Then a few flashes of memory came back to him, being summoned by a magical cry for help, Kalleth's rebellion, and he recalled his capture and being marched into the obsidian stronghold, but then his memory went blank. Bruinen could not recollect any spells or incantations, no runes, potion recipes, not even the word for fire! For an old wizard who had been subjected to many things he was starting to detest the cramped, and icy, prison cell. A shiver ran from his scalp to his finger tips. He was seated on a simple cot, and the only other feature of the cell was a small window to his left. Through the bars, he could just barely make out a glowing torch. The small wisp of warmth which radiated from the window made Bruinen sigh. He yearned to grow closer to the fire, to let its heat engulf him, to become the fire itself, to ignite. He gasped, looking down at his hands, "Ignaros," he whispered, gazing in wonder as a small spark flew from his hand. "I-Ignaros!" he said, louder, drawing on his life force to strengthen the spell. A flame coalesced in his hand, as a similarly fiery grin spread across Bruinen's features.

Several hours later, after picking through his memory with mixed results, Bruinen felt exhausted and needed sleep. Soon he was startled awake by a loud shriek. He sat up on his cot, his ears straining to hear more. The sound of glass shattering made him jump, and he slid off his bed, landing on the cold stone floor. Peering out of his window, Bruinen couldn't see much more than the glow of the torch. A loud *bang!* sounded from several feet away, and a raspy growl accompanied by the stench of rotting flesh assaulted Bruinen's senses. The taste of bile rose in his throat, and he stumbled backward as a pit of anxiety grew in his chest. "Pierce the flesh, burn the skin. Rend the bone, KILL BRUINEN!" A horrible voice whispered and began to cough wetly. Bruinen scowled and pulled himself to his feet. Clearing his throat, he looked up at the ceiling. "Terros Fallan Vhairnouros!" (Make Falling Stone Bring Death!) he exclaimed, not quite knowing how he had remembered the incantation. Pressing himself up against the back wall of his cell Bruinen watched in fascination as a crack quivered into being, and slowly spread, until it spider-webbed across the entire ceiling. In the same moment his cell door opened, the executioner's stench preceded the beast into the prison cell. Suddenly, a massive section of the ceiling crashed down and his gruesome assailant screamed in shock. Bruinen had effectively crushed the threat of his assassin. The old potion master dodged the falling rubble and stumbled over the pile of debris. Reaching the corridor, he quickly escaped before anyone or anything could capture him and stumbled off in search of his nephews.

"Who are you?" Pain rippled across Ezekiel's cheek as a muscular man, wearing a turban and thick robes, punched him ferociously. The abuse had gone on for what seemed like hours. His captor would ask him questions, most of which he could not answer. Then, at Ezekiel's silence, he would endure ever more creative and painful torture. However, the most terrifying part was that despite the pain he felt, he never bled, burned, suffocated, or broke. "Why are you doing this?" Ezekiel pleaded, writhing in the ropes that bound him. "I ask the questions!" was the response, and a powerful kick launched Ezekiel across the room. It became apparent to him, that his mysterious tormentor was not entirely human. Ezekiel was a heavily muscled knight, and one does not simply throw that kind of weight across the room. "I suppose, given the circumstances I'll answer your question" the turbaned tyrant replied. Ezekiel could feel the man's warm breath in his ear, "But only because I want to." He gave Ezekiel a powerful uppercut, effectively silencing any reply from his victim. Out of the corner of his eye Ezekiel watched as his captor walked towards him with the confident strides of someone who has won a battle. One thought echoed in Ezekiel's mind: *please let this be the end of me! Please!*

"Tell me your name!" yelled the man. Ezekiel glanced upward, to find the man holding him at sword point, with a menacing gleam in his eyes. "Be assured, you will most certainly feel the pain of death if you do not cooperate." Ezekiel felt an insurmountable defeat rising up his throat, and he only just managed to choke out, "Ezekiel... Bright-Talon."

"Tell me your name!" yelled Alwyck.

The Trap

Sweat ran into Verin's eyes, the salty liquid burning and blurring his vision. He urged Kalleth forward, beckoning for him to follow. "Come! Quickly!" cried Verin, noting his cousin's distress. Kalleth was beginning to worry about their situation. Upon leaving the elevator, the cousins found themselves standing on a barren plain, dotted with ruins, and sparse plant life. Without warning they were ambushed as hundreds of ferocious gargoyles with vicious fangs raced towards them. Clearly incapable of defeating the throng, Verin chose to seek cover in a small charred shack, and hurried towards the structure, not heeding the shouted warnings from Kalleth. "Look out!" his cousin cried as spikes shot from hidden orifices behind shrubbery and boulders. Verin called on Ignaros, and a jet of white-hot flame melted the spikes into blunt stumps. "Why would a prison be so treacherous in design, and who would ever want to work here?" questioned Kalleth, as he watched an unlucky gargoyle become impaled by an unmelted spike. Verin's response came fast, as the half-blood demon ducked and dodged through the newest obstacle: arcane lightning! "This part of the prison must be reserved for offenders so hated and traitorous that the guards simply dump them here to die." Verin dove beneath a lava-rock outcropping, and conjured a spell to shield them, as Kalleth replied, "But, these are obviously traps, and why are there buildings outside?" Verin explained, "A long time ago, the 'outside' was inside, and demons roamed free. However, when the great invasions occurred on earth, the customs of mortals were adopted and evolved into what you see before you. Humanity has had a great effect on us." Verin hastily corrected himself, "I mean *them*." Looking down he flinched at the sight of a bestial skull, and he kicked the wall in growing frustration for their lack of progress in finding Ezekiel and Bruinen. Much to his surprise the floor crumbled away, revealing a passageway below. Kalleth observed that the walls were fashioned from lapis lazuli, the precious deep blue stone that was flecked with gold. Gilded archways held up the roof. "Ahhh!" came a cry from within. Kalleth and Verin looked at each other simultaneously, recognizing the voice as their Uncle Bruinen. Scrambling inside, they were oblivious to the light footfalls of a turban-clad figure slinking after them.

Bruinen crept through the alley-like halls of this strange realm, he had been able to remember a few protective spells and had cast an incantation of invisibility so that he was safely concealed from view. Every few minutes, more vivid memories of spells, and enchantments seeped back into his brain. A suspicion rose within him that perhaps the sabotage of his abilities was only temporary. *However, until I remember everything, I am at a huge disadvantage!* Bruinen thought, cursing his misfortune. He paused beneath a windowsill to catch his breath. The sign by the door marked this building as an old pub. Gathering himself to move on, Bruinen started to creep forward but something stopped him. A muttered question filtered out the window of the pub. "So, where's Alwyck off to now?" Bruinen crouched under the window, listening intently. Another voice sounded, "He claims to have found the boss's other son, you know the half-blood freak." What the speaker could not know, was that the "freak's" uncle was hiding beneath the window sill trembling with fury, barely able to control himself as he continued to eavesdrop. The speaker continued uneasily, "And apparently Alwyck is looking to punish his brother for betraying his family." He lowered his voice, encouraging his companion to listen closer, "There are rumours, that Dazra has turned to the light, and that our newly captured prisoners will be set free. While others believe," his voice dropping further to a low whisper, "that Alwyck is plotting to usurp the throne and destroy Zarym Malic altogether." Suddenly the window sill exploded into splinters as a hellish skeleton wielding a menacing axe cleaved through the sill. Bruinen had been discovered. "Show yourself!" the guard commanded in a raspy croak. Running full speed for an escape Bruinen felt little remorse for the patron, whose gossip had proven so helpful, even if the telling had cost him his life. *This news might just have tipped the scales in our favor*, thought Bruinen. *Verin, I'm coming!*

"Kalleth! Stop! It's a traaa-mmff!" Ezekiel's voice was cut off and he felt gagged by an invisible force before he could finish yelling out a warning to his brother. The warning came too late. Ezekiel looked on in horror as Kalleth leapt over a black pit and fell through the floor. Suddenly, Kalleth was suspended into the air sharing the same fate as Ezekiel: trapped, held captive in a heavy metal cage. From his vantage point Ezekiel could see a second man, one with reptilian features teetering on the ledge, as he heard the creature gasp in disbelief, "Gods, it's a trap!"

Cold, cruel laughter echoed through the chamber and sent chills down Verin's spine. The sound seemed to emanate through the walls. "Bravo, Bright-Talon clan, you have made the foolish mistake of gathering in one spot. How convenient. Now it will be easier for me to kill you all at once!" The scaly stranger, whose claws were not capable of gripping the smooth cavern walls, growled in rage. "Alwyck, how dare you kidnap my friends? You and I are family, why do you insist on spreading chaos and wreaking havoc?" The wall shimmered with magic, and from within emerged a tall, slender, man with exotic features and sun-bronzed skin. He was garbed in expensive robes and a turban, and was wielding a wicked looking scythe. The blade seemed to gleam brighter in anticipation of the taste of blood. In a deathly quiet whisper, Alwyck replied, "I am chaos incarnate." A howl tore from his lips, and he raised his weapon. "My dear half-brother, you seem to be having trouble with your corporeal form, let me help!" He swung his scythe, and the dragon-like man fell to the floor, curled in a fetal position. Immediately, Verin's body erupted into hives which at the slightest movement burst, streaming noxious pus. Within seconds of bursting, more hives formed. Verin thrashed in pain, the virulent white substance burning him. Ezekiel, who had fought in many bloody battles, was overwhelmed by nausea, and averted his eyes. Alwyck turned his attention to Kalleth, and a sadistic expression settled on his features clearly visible beneath his turbaned brow.

"Verin!" Kalleth cried out, watching the affliction with horrified fascination. Suddenly, from the corner of his eye his attention was drawn to a small blue pebble that had skittered across the floor at the base of the staircase. However, he had no time to pursue that thought, because the satanic lord taunted him from below. "Kalleth, you seem like a trustworthy person, so let me tell you a secret. Bruinen is dead." With a flourish of his scythe, Alwyck revealed a battered corpse. Within his cramped cage Kalleth fell to his knees, tears welling in his eyes. His own tutor, a trusted friend, and beloved uncle, dead? "No! Impossible, it must be an illusion. Bruinen cannot be dead." Alwyck looked him over with interest, "Why so scared, you are just pathetic!" Kalleth smiled fiercely, taking a deep breath. "Because your brother is about to beat you senseless!" Alwyck jumped back in shock, and whipped around to see Verin still curled on the floor. "A trick!" he hissed, turning back to the cage from which Kalleth was now absent. The diversion had given Kalleth enough time to conceal himself with a cover spell. Barely able to contain his frustration Alwyck scoured the chamber for his rebellious prisoner. A small question puzzled Kalleth: why was he able to use his magic now when the netherworld had blocked him before? "What a joke!" Thought Kalleth. Taking deep, even breaths he focused on happier times. His vision faded into deep royal purple, which rippled and moved like a violet ocean. He looked up to see the purple-robed lady sitting in a silver throne. "I see you are in need of a gift."

Bruinen could hear voices up ahead and peeked around the corner. He had nearly cried out as he watched Verin writhing in pain. Backing up the stairwell, he searched for some kind of distraction. He scanned the lapis walls and spied a small pebble which would work perfectly. He fidgeted with the pebble nervously as he readied himself for action. *I still can't remember all the spells!* he thought worriedly. However, strengthening his resolve, he thought about Verin lying tortured on the ground because of that monster.

Bruinen crept down the stairs and into the chamber, concealing himself with a spell as he moved into place. Unfortunately, he had not anticipated that casting the spell would drain him of what small energy reserves he possessed after being imprisoned and abused for so long. Suddenly, Bruinen's vision blurred as he fell unconscious upon the floor. The small blue pebble bounced and skittered to a halt at his feet.

The Visions

The moment he was struck by the illness, Verin feared that the fight was over. He lost control as pain wracked his body. Shuddering and convulsing, he couldn't perceive anything beyond the horrible fire that burned every inch of his skin. He began to retreat into a dark corner of his mind, to find shelter from the powerful sensations bombarding him. By some twist of fate, though, he remembered the cloud ring and thrust his oozing hand into his pocket. Finding the ring in Svatan's courtyard had seemed like it had happened a lifetime ago. By some strange impulse he forced the small iron and gold band onto his swollen finger. Verin sucked in his breath, fighting panic as his mind was torn from the dark cavernous prison into the outside world, his vision expanded to encompass the prison chamber, then stretched beyond the outside plains, and then even farther. He seemed to be flying through space and time. Verin tried to focus his mind back into his body, but he was lost in a black void. He looked to his right, and glimpsed a cloudy pantheon on top of a rocky bluff. Then turned his gaze to the left, where he recognized his father's obsidian fortress. Most puzzling to be sure was what happened when he looked straight ahead; he could see the familiar pine forest that was home to his uncle's cabin. A hammer blow pounded his ribs and pulled his consciousness back down towards the prison, but before he left his magical vision he turned just in time to see a silvery steed with golden-feathered wings bearing a fierce warrior into battle. The warrior's eyes met with his, and in that moment he saw Kalleth's calm but determined gaze.

FOOD, WINE AND GOLD COVERED ALMOST EVERY SURFACE.

Intense focus and an unknown mystical force transported Kalleth beyond the restraints of his cage into another realm. Kalleth couldn't find his voice, surrounded by extravagance as he was. Long tables were scattered around the hall, groaning under the weight of their burdens. Food, wine and gold covered almost every surface. What little floor space that remained appeared to be polished marble, and the columns were inlaid with gold and other precious stones.

Kalleth cautiously approached a circle of thrones, only one of which was not broken and abandoned. To the right of the centre seat, was a silvery chair, adorned in vines, which had been set slightly outside the circle. Much to his surprise comfortably enthroned before him sat the mysterious lady in purple robes. "I see you are heavily burdened and in need." Kalleth nodded, "My friends have been injured and are trapped!" The goddess hushed him, and caressed his face. "This is a big decision, and time moves differently here, so calm yourself and listen to me." Kalleth sighed in relief and slumped to the ground with his back leaning against an old throne. The purple-clad woman gathered her robes around her and with a small wave, lit a fire in the hearth. "As this circle of broken thrones reveals mortals have followed in this path of destruction before, but regretfully," gesturing towards the empty chairs, "many have died painfully before their time." The goddess' face fell, "And I alone remain." Kalleth frowned, "The food and the riches?" The purple-robed lady laughed bitterly. "A simple illusion, left by a former master, meant to impress on visitors an appearance of greatness where none remains." She waved a hand, which passed through a sparkling sapphire in her armrest. She cleared her throat and turned to Kalleth. "In any event, you must make a very important choice. I will grant my powers unto you, but the cost to your physical body may very well kill you." Kalleth closed his eyes, his brow furrowed in thought. "Before I make my choice I need to know that there's hope. Show me my friends!" he cried out. The goddess opened her mouth as if to speak, but then silenced her thought. She reached forward and with an index finger, she gently touched his forehead. At once, his vision clouded and he was transported to yet another place. Although it wasn't to his friends in the prison cavern. Instead, the vision he saw puzzled him. A balding man in black robes sat under a willow tree, eating an apple. Two figures approached, one a leper and the other a colorful jester. The leper knelt before the man and begged for healing. The robed man agreed and raised his hands. An ebony ribbon extended towards the leper and morphed into a sash. It writhed over the leper's skin and miraculously, he was healed. On the other hand the jester made a humble plea for money to feed his family. Which was a lie for he had spent his entire life as a hired assassin. Kalleth watched as the balding man shouted, "May the demons that employed you be damned!" With a flourish, he loosed a tendril of dark cloth that quickly smothered the jester causing his gruesome death. In the same instant the black robed man fell to his knees as his robe began to smoke and shredded into ribbons which began to flame, the man's back arched in pain, and what hair he had left fell to the ground. His black robe had completely burned up, and the man who had once stood confident and proud, now lay dead beneath the willow tree. Somehow time seemed to speed up, and the willow tree withered and sulked. In the same instant the fog seemed to clear from Kalleth's mind.

Kalleth opened his eyes and found the goddess crying. He jumped up and went to her side. "My name, my real name, is Aeyri." Now he finally knew the identity of the mysterious purple robed lady who had been a constant and sometimes annoying presence in his mind over the past few months. Aeyri held her face in her hands. "So many gods from the pantheon have been lost as a result of mankind's foolishness!" At first Kalleth hesitated, but then overcome with compassion he brushed the tears from Aeyri's cheek. He spoke softly saying, "I've made my decision, but I have to ask, have you made yours?" She looked up, and gave him a smile that didn't reach her eyes. "There is no way I could watch this travesty unfold and not offer you my assistance! We have to stop Alwyck, or the balance of the universe will be upset and all will be lost!" Kalleth also smiled, but knew deep down that the situation was dire. Grabbing her hand, Kalleth led her to the edge of the temple and asked, "Now, how do we accomplish this task?" Aeyri clasped his hand and turned to face him. "When you exit your meditation in the spirit state, I'll be with you." Kalleth was so inspired by this brave and courageous woman, that he started to experience feelings he had long thought lost. Kalleth knelt at Aeyri's feet and kissed her hand. "See you on the other side!" he called as he dove off the precipice. Aeyri seemed enamoured of the valiant knight. She smiled shyly, shook her head, and mounted her winged steed.

Chronicle Five: The Three Realms Unite

The Redemption

Alwyck's twisted desire to inflict torture became even more apparent when Ezekiel awoke from heat exhaustion only to find himself still imprisoned. Ezekiel was chained to a ledge, which hung several thousand feet above a flaming pit. In addition, the fiery hole held darkened shapes which clambered over each other and appeared to be howling at the scent of Ezekiel's fear. The fiery beasts resembled dogs, yet remained nebulous and unseen in the roiling liquid. While Ezekiel struggled against his bonds, his face reflected such a strong expression of hatred that Alwyck stepped back in caution. Chuckling to himself the demon was enjoying his victim's predicament. Ezekiel started, when Alwyck addressed him. "You seem to be in a bit of a bind. Let me help you." Ezekiel's eyes narrowed and he searched for some sort of deceit or trickery, in the demon's eyes. "You don't trust me?" Alwyck gasped in mock distress. With a disapproving tut, he unveiled Ezekiel's sword, which the brave knight had all but abandoned hope of ever seeing again. "See? I'm perfectly trustworthy!" the fiend grinned, and dangled the weapon over the pit. Ezekiel smiled in response to Alwyck's threat and replied, "The dog should not bite the hand that feeds it." Alwyck pronounced with a scowl. "What are you talking about?" Ezekiel spat at his captor, who roared and dropped the sword. Ezekiel almost lost his weapon, but at the last second managed to hook the sword between his boots. Unable to free his hands, he cursed his misfortune and inched Varkath to safety, bracing the sword between his legs. In the same moment a haunting cry echoed from across the plains, and he saw Alwyck's face contort into an expression of amazed confusion.

When Verin returned to his body he was blind. His flesh was swollen beyond any human recognition, and he was deaf and ignorant of his surroundings. After what seemed like several hours passed, he felt a miraculous healing sensation. The hives began to shrink, the pus flowed away and his senses began to return. However, what he saw next left him staring in disbelief. Standing before him was a newly transformed Kalleth. He looked years younger. His posture was straighter, his muscles more defined, and he seemed ramped up and ready for anything. "How do you feel?" Kalleth asked, pulling him upright. Verin smiled, "Almost back to myself. How did you heal my affliction?" he asked, stretching his stiff joints. Kalleth's expression grew darker, "I removed Alwyck's curse, but the real secret of your healing is mine to know. Can we leave your questions unanswered for the time being?" Their reunion was cut short when they suddenly heard a clash of steel on rock, and Verin cried out, "Where is Ezekiel? We must find him!" Without warning a hand grabbed Verin's shoulder, and he twisted around in shock, to see a very familiar face. "Uncle!" Verin and Kalleth cried out in unison. Verin clapped Bruinen on the shoulder, and brought the old man into a bear hug. "How did you escape the prison?" Bruinen chuckled at them, "O ye of little faith. Unfortunately I was drugged, my powers have only now begun to return." He turned to Kalleth, and his face was transformed by suspicion, "You seem...different." He stepped closer, noting his nephew's height. "You're taller, is there something you haven't told me?" Kalleth laughed nervously, but backed away. "I'm sorry, uncle, but I can't tell you without risking someone else's life." Bruinen gasped, but joy lit his face. "Could it be?" he asked cryptically, more to himself than to Kalleth. Then he shrugged and gestured to Verin, "Let's go!" Verin couldn't help but feel that they were keeping something secret from him. Unfortunately, a bloodcurdling howl pushed every thought to the back of his mind.

———•◆•———

Bruinen rushed up the spiral staircase alongside his nephews. They searched for the source of the frightening howl, and spotted Alwyck, at some distance away, gazing down with great interest. "Let's see if we can catch him by surprise," whispered Kalleth, crouching. The others followed suit and soon the trio were concealed behind a small boulder near the cliff's edge. Bruinen heard Alwyck roar, and carefully peeked around the rock, in time to watch as the devil wiped Ezekiel's spittle from his face in disgust. A smile curved Bruinen's mouth at the thought of Ezekiel's defiance, even in the face of death. Truly though, the

Bright-Talon family had landed themselves in a big mess from which Bruinen wasn't so sure they could escape. Too many times the old potion master had cheated death but this time felt different, Bruinen thought grimly. He had a strong suspicion that eventually their luck would run out. Suddenly, the hell-raising screech they'd heard returned and sounded much closer and full of vengeance. The ground shook, and a quick glance told them that Alwyck was just as surprised as they were. Astonishingly the cave beyond the rocky outcropping exploded, sending debris high into the air. Smoke billowed from what remained of the cave, and heavy footsteps sent the fauna of the nether realm running for cover. Bats with fiery wings and three-headed moles scurried in terror from the unseen threat. The following chaos was amplified by a hellish chorus echoing from the fire pit. Kalleth stared amazed that the cacophony which had erupted from the fiery hole was even louder than the noise made by the unseen monster. Bruinen chose that moment to reveal himself to his enemy. If Alwyck was surprised by this new situation, his expression didn't give anything away. Verin's turbaned half-brother threw back his head and howled. The noise raised the hairs on Bruinen's neck and his feet seemed glued to the spot. In response to the howling call, a huge geyser of magma issued from the pit, propelling the hellhounds that had skulked within. The pack of canine beasts swarmed around Alwyck, at first appearing to attack him, when in truth he appeared to be commanding them. Bruinen and his nephews had suffered throughout their journey in the nether-realm because of the dark and toxic environment. Yet now, the clouds of gas parted, and the strangest moon shone through, leaving its radiance to filter through the searing fumes, and bathing the grey heath in a stain of blood-red light.

As if the fountains of lava and hellhounds weren't enough, Ezekiel could sense his strength flagging. First one finger, then two, and finally he lost his grip, tumbling into the fiery pit below. The chain binding him had long since melted, and Ezekiel's body was riddled with burns. He kicked away from the cliff, resigned to his fast approaching end. Sword in hand, he closed his eyes. High above him, the mysterious beast from the cave erupted. With surprising speed and agility, the dark form plummeted straight towards him and plucked Ezekiel from the air effectively stopping his fall. Fragrant smoke billowed from his liberator's ample snout, coating the knight's already badly damaged armour. Just as quickly as he had been rescued he was unceremoniously dropped beside his friends next to the boulder. Evidently the magnificent dragon, despite spewing ashen smoke, could also transport objects with incredible gentleness and accuracy. Together at last, the Bright-Talon family prepared to face their enemy.

 Alwyck had turned an amusing shade of purple, but Ezekiel couldn't decide whether it was burgundy or violet, perhaps a combination of the two. His evil brother's tone however, was far from humorous. "Damn you Bright-Talon scum!" he sneered under his breath, and Verin would have sworn that he saw smoke escaping from Alwyck's beet-red ears. Astonishingly, several of the flaming dogs positioned themselves to create a makeshift throne. "No matter how I have tried to usurp total control of the universe, you blasted mortals have foiled my plans!" Bruinen stepped forward and pried a brittle root from the earth, remarking in a clear strong voice, "We have never intruded upon your lands, devil. It was you who has continually invaded our realm. Furthermore you are responsible for driving fear into the hearts of our people and slaughtering countless innocents!" his expression grew even more fierce as he continued. "Nay, you cannot begin to beg pardon for your sins, not when I stand before you bearing a gift!" He knelt before Alwyck and carefully planted the root into the dry, barren soil. From his sleeve, Bruinen produced a small vial, and quickly removed the stopper. Before anyone could react, the wizard poured the vial over the root, and a bluish-green liquid covered the plant and seeped into the ground. Alwyck was outraged when he caught the scent of his blood, and even more so, when he saw Bruinen exploiting the liquid for his own magic.

Ezekiel tumbled into the fiery pit.

The Epic Battle

Kalleth was curious how Bruinen had managed to conceal the wraith's blood when everything else had been confiscated. However, now they faced a bigger challenge. Even as the last drop fell, Alwyck roared commands to his hounds, his veins pulsing at his temple. In response the hounds leapt towards the root. Quickly swelling in size Kalleth was stunned to see the plant growing so rapidly. Vines lashed out and strangled any of the hounds who got too close. Blooms and fruit also hastily appeared. The surrounding ground appeared to come alive with activity and was covered in a thick carpet of thick green grass and a multitude of flowers. Alwyck screamed and cried out until his voice cracked. Suddenly, from behind the evil menace rose an intimidating silhouette, with three pairs of glowing eyes. The moon was obscured by the body of the giant dragon flying to their aid. Flames shot from the creature's mouth and illuminated Alwyck's newest weapon. Alwyck turned and leapt into the hollow between his mysterious steed's three necks. "Seems as though we ought to get on with the fight!" Aeryi's thought echoed in Kalleth's head, dripping sarcasm. Kalleth shook his head, for he was becoming accustomed to her caustic mental comments by now. He reached for his weapon and was surprised to find nothing on his hip. He had forgotten that his bow was still locked up somewhere in the obsidian fortress. "What ever would you do without me?" the goddess sighed, wondering to herself how they had forgotten to make a side trip to the armoury. She conjured a bow laced with silver vines, and carved from oak, which suddenly appeared in Kalleth's hand. A similarly fashioned quiver appeared out of thin air strapped across his chest. However, Kalleth noticed the arrows were oddly shaped. Kalleth quickly examined one of the arrows even as he prepared to shoot. The shaft was fashioned from blackened stone, which was threaded throughout with veins of red, gold, and orange. He thought he must have been losing his mind because he could have sworn the tips were cut from diamond. "Aye, the tips are cut from diamond, but the shaft is made of pyreroot, which ignites when moving at high velocity, so scorch him in his sweet spot Kalleth!" teased Aeryi.

THREE LONG NECKS HELD THREE FRIGHTENING HEADS, THAT OF A COBRA, WOLF, AND LION.

A grin spread across his face, which soon fell away when he sized up his intimidating foe. Three long necks held three frightening heads, that of a cobra, wolf, and lion. These were unbelievably fused onto a body which appeared to be an amalgamation of all three predators. The heads screeched in unison, the piercing sound driving Kalleth and his friends to their knees. Kalleth stood up again, and aiming down the sight of his bow, loosed an arrow and withdrew another in record time. True to Aeyri's word, the missile ignited at the peak of its arc and found its mark with a flash. The lion recoiled in pain, contracting the other heads at the same time. Kalleth let two more arrows fly, grazing the neck of the wolf but missing the serpent. A foul scent of melting hair assaulted his nostrils, making him gag. He stole a backwards glance to the others, and the smell of burnt hair quickly became the least of his worries.

Verin stood amazed by Kalleth's accuracy with a bow. Suddenly, he felt the hair on his neck prickle as a blast of hot air warmed his back. He turned in shock to see the smoking beast. A dragon, with coal black scales and red markings, was looming above him. This alone would have been enough to put even a half-blood on edge, but what shocked him more deeply was what he observed on the dragon's head. Indeed there was only one brilliant red horn, atop the beasts head the other sharpened spike was missing! "Father!" Verin cried out, unsure whether to run from him or embrace the giant reptile. The massive creature lowered his head towards Verin. "Why are you here?" he attempted to ask, not understanding his father's benevolent behavior. Zarym's powerful voice hit his mind like a sledgehammer. "I am here to right a wrong. Son, you may not have been as obedient as I might have wished, but you never betrayed me!" As the weight of his father's words sunk in, Verin watched the dragon's talons ripping the earth and a rumbling growl was heard. "I now realize I will never become the king of all realms. However, I would like to regain control of my own!" he nearly roared. Verin nodded his assent. Kalleth's labored breathing brought Verin quickly back into focus as he hurriedly added, "Father help us! My cousin grows weary, and Alwyck's strength is growing stronger by the minute." The dragon's remaining horn glowed blood red as he rose to his full height. "Time to teach that brat to respect his elders!"

Ezekiel ran to his brother's side, his sword drawn. *I must redeem myself!* he thought, cringing at the tortures he had suffered and his futile efforts to warn them of Alwyck's trap. From his seat between the cobra and the wolf, Verin's older brother leered at them, spewing poisonous insults with bewildering speed. "Ah, will you boys never tire? I must apologize, you haven't been properly introduced to my dear pet!" Alwyck's "pet" as he called the monstrosity was frothing from all three mouths, and pulling against the chain. He tapped the creature's heads in quick succession, tutting with disapproval. "Now Gazyx, behave! We have guests! We only kill them after explaining the futility of their existence!" Alwyck scolded the terrifying scourge as though it were a young child. Gazyx responded by lurching forward in a renewed attack on the brothers. Ezekiel pushed Kalleth out of harm's way, his sword gleaming as he deflected the viper's fangs. The wolf stalked behind the lion, who unleashed a deafening roar. With a cry of rage, the lion fell upon Ezekiel, tossing and turning its massive head, blow for blow. Ezekiel skillfully parried each of the lion's attacks. Just as he had settled into a fighting rhythm and sweat began to wet his brow, he suddenly screamed, arching his back in pain, as without warning the wolf's serrated teeth tore into his leg. The lion withdrew to allow the massive wolf the chance to kill. In shock from the pain of his injury, Ezekiel's battle-lust increased to a point where his senses expanded beyond what seemed humanly possible. He sensed a subtle shift in the air behind his right ear and instantly reacted by twisting his body to the left. Ezekiel quickly raised his sword just as the wolf's giant head launched an attack. Barely having enough time to react, his canine foe adjusted its lunge in an ill-met attempt to evade Ezekiel's weapon. Varkath, his sword, grazed the wolf, effectively shaving the right side of its face. Finally managing to halt its forward momentum the wolf withdrew, whimpering. Kalleth laughed at his brother's excellent combat prowess, which sent hope rising in Ezekiel's chest. A well aimed arrow pierced the wolf's remaining eye, and the monstrous head sunk with a gurgle. A victorious scream escaped Alwyck's lips, incongruous after witnessing the wolf's death. "Brace yourselves!" Bruinen yelled out, fumbling with some powders and herbs.

Bruinen was nearly finished with the incantations when he saw the storm clouds approach. A wall of heavy black was tearing down the plains with demonic speed. The wind began to howl, and a strange light shone from within the clouds. Immediately, Bruinen recognized the spell, shouting in panic, "Prepare your weapons!" Then all of a sudden, the combined armies of the hell dimension appeared adorned as they were in onyx armour. Thundering across the plains, the deafening cry of, "AV TOR NOS NETHRAKOS LYCAN!" (We swear Allegiance to Hell's Shadow!) echoed as the pulsing throng of demons swore fealty to Hell's Shadow. Their dragon master roared, and the mass of reinforcements charged towards Alwyck. However, something was afoot, as hundreds of the demons began to falter. Bruinen watched in disbelief as they stopped in their tracks and without warning turned to fight against their allies and began to cut them down. Seeing this travesty, Zarym Malic cried out, feeling the pain of each loss. High above the battlefield the magnificent dragon flew attempting to identify the rebels, but there were too many carefully concealed soldiers stealing through the ranks, bloodletting and causing bedlam. When the soldiers faithful to Zarym Malic finally regrouped, their numbers had been devastated; at least one-third were dead, and another third had turned against them. Alwyck scowled at the small group of rebels, that were now surrounded by his warriors, jeering at them. "Hide me," Bruinen whispered, addressing his nephews. They obediently encircled their uncle safeguarding him from the ensuing chaos.

BRUINEN WAS POURING HIS LIFE FORCE INTO THE TINY SAPLING.

Bruinen feverishly knelt over the tiny tree. Unknown to his circle of protection, he was pouring his life force into the tiny sapling. Bruinen raised an eyebrow as he considered the likelihood that this action might hasten his death. His gaze turned to his brave friends, family, and brothers-in-arms. The ancient mage knew his absence would devastate them. However, he felt this action was the only path he could choose.

Verin was curious about what his uncle was planning, yet obeyed his uncle's command. No matter what Bruinen had up his sleeve, Verin was not feeling optimistic about their chances. Zarym Malic's faithful servants had been crushed, but even as the enemy began to close in on the Bright-Talons, they heard a war-cry. Zarym Malic had rallied what troops remained, and they charged into the fray. In a valiant effort, the battle began anew. Alwyck's brutes were being forced inward. With the outcome of battle finally turning in Zarym Malic's favour, Verin took a moment and turned to face Bruinen. "No!" Verin cried out, falling to his knees, as he understood his uncle's plan. "Why did you sacrifice yourself?" He looked to his cousins for help. However, Kalleth and Ezekiel had already left the circle and were joining the fight, cutting down demons. Bruinen wheezed, "I'll be fine, trust me!" He touched his nephew's arm. "Now go, help them!"

Verin acquiesced and raised his war hammer. He had made a vow to protect the old wizard at all costs. Many fierce demons were destroyed by the Bright-Talon trio, who were systematically cutting them down by the dozens. However, in the same instant Gazyx's remaining two heads focused on them and pounced, attacking from both sides. Kalleth grunted, rapier pressed against him, as the viper hissed in anger and began to coil around him. Ezekiel glanced back and, seeing his brother in trouble, slammed the big cat's head with his boot. With a flourish, revealing his years of experience with a blade, Ezekiel quickly dispatched the serpent. Much to his shock, the venom-filled glands in the dead beast began to explode, spraying corrosive poison everywhere. The knight recoiled in panic, violently wiping away the liquid. Although he managed to prevent most of the damage, his left eye had become dangerously swollen.

With his visibility reduced by half, Ezekiel cursed his fate but forged ahead into combat. He thought about how to shield his blind spot, deciding he would have to rely on his other senses to survive. Summoning a deep focus from within he began to listen carefully to his surroundings, hearing the clamour of battle as never before. Suddenly, the lion's head returned, ducking and weaving, all the while emitting a roar fit to wake the dead. Ezekiel responded with a flurry of jabs and swipes, tracking the monster with his good eye. At one point he lost his footing, thrown off his equilibrium by his injured eye, and rolled onto his back. Immediately, the six inch fangs plunged towards Ezekiel's head, however moments before they would have torn open his exposed jugular vein, the creature pulled back. Ezekiel was vexed by this devil's cruelty. "If you are going to kill me, do it with honour, you foul, wretched thing!" In truth, he was angry that everything had come to this.

Ezekiel was vexed by Alwyck's cruelty.

Ezekiel Bright-Talon, King of Autumn Castle and the surrounding lands, had failed. He had used every ounce of his energy to fight against this hell, only to be bested in the end! Why? Quite suddenly however, he was filled by a new sensation, an unquenchable thirst for battle permeated his brain, and then just as suddenly, his mind went blank. He charged forward, sword outstretched and already covered with blood. He leapt onto the fused torso of the beast, "You know, that wasn't a very bright idea." Alwyck sneered. The demon cackled, and in one fluid motion twisted, and landed a powerful blow to his prey. What remained of Ezekiel's vision darkened and blurred with the force of the hit. Blind bloodlust fueled his attack, and the king lost track of time, it might have been minutes or hours that passed as the duo fought. History books would record that there was never a closer brawl between demon and mortal since. Eventually Alwyck, drenched in sweat, scored a lucky hit. Ezekiel's armor, battered and broken, clanged against the hard earth as the defeated king fell to the ground.

The Sacrifice

Kalleth felt sick to his stomach, an all too familiar situation. He and Verin were back to back, fending off blow after blow. "Got any other ideas on how we might get out of this situation alive?" the half-blood shouted behind him. Kalleth felt Aeyri's presence pushing up against his mind in an attempt to unleash her powers. "I might have a few," he answered, a grim smile on his lips. "Are you sure? Using my powers might kill you." Kalleth ignored Aeyri's cautioning plea and raised a hand. "Oltari Deose Illumai!" (Blind My Enemies with Light!) The goddess' power blinded the attackers, and gave the two cousins a momentary advantage and time to fight back. In that same moment a small seed of hope rose in their hearts. Suddenly, the unthinkable happened. Alwyck, the betrayer took to the air riding Gazyx upwards targeting the dragon, Zarym Malic. With a malicious glint in his eyes Alwyck stabbed his father through the heart. Oddly, the great creature made no noise, falling limply to the ground. Unexpectedly, Verin collapsed onto his knees, experiencing telepathically the mortal wounding of his father with excruciating pain. Kalleth knelt beside his cousin and quickly helped him up, before running towards Alwyck he yelled back to Verin, "Take care of your father! I must end this chaos!"

Verin leapt into the black cavern of the monster's gaping jaw.

Verin felt a strange sense of composure despite the pounding ache in his head. He certainly had been devastated by seeing his father's fall, but duty and the lives of so many innocents became his priority. There would be time to grieve later, if he didn't end up in the grave himself! So, with a flick of his wrist and a wink, he sprinted toward Gazyx. The lion turned toward him, hissing. Ignoring the beast's warning, Verin ran to the devil's feet. An enthusiastic screech of delight erupted from the monster's huge maw. Verin thought to himself that he must be crazy, his plan was insane, this idea couldn't possibly work. Verin's thoughts were interrupted by two rows of pearly white fangs, which might as well have been swords, looming over him. He cringed, and jumped upward, every fibre of his being crying out for him to stop.

Propelling himself forward, he dove into the blackness of the monster's feline jaws.

"You fool!" Bruinen moaned softly to himself, kneeling beside the now-fully grown oak tree. He had only a whisper of life energy left flowing through his body. He was surprised by the next thought which occurred to him, his death had been predestined for this time, but how could he have known the stakes would be so high? Nonetheless, he knew his duty, and without so much as a grunt he got to his feet. The last piece of magic he'd worked, was a simple wooden staff which he had leaned against the tree trunk. He picked up the staff, and walked towards his destiny. Kalleth was hiding behind a partially destroyed wall, his bow drawn. Alwyck was firing bolts of electricity over his head and the air fizzled loudly. The demon paused to recover energy. Kalleth took his chance and loosed arrow after arrow at his foe. Fire engulfed Alwyck as each arrow met its mark. "Curse you, you wretched fools, I'm immune to fire!" he yelled. Kalleth smirked, "Well, it doesn't seem to be an enjoyable experience!" As he leapt forward and thrust a powerful beam of light through Alwyck's chest, which was accompanied by Aeyri's ringing laugh. Sadly, Bruinen knew the blow wasn't enough to destroy Alwyck. Bruinen continued towards his intended target. A warning rumble came from Gazyx, further disorienting his cruel master. Suddenly, Verin's fist exploded from within the Lion's neck and the beast recoiled in pain. Covered in slimy gore Verin tore open the beast's flesh, his war hammer flying. Bruinen sucked in a breath and cried out. "Verin, jump!" Confused, his nephew looked back but he obeyed the command. Raising his staff, Bruinen charged and struck Alwyck in the head. Then several things happened at once. Gazyx, the monstrous beast tumbled to the ground, causing the earth to quake. A huge section of the ground fell away, dropping into an abyss. Fear briefly touched the old mage's heart. However, he had placed his faith in this plan and there was no going back now. Bruinen vigorously swung his staff a second time, praying that his strategy would work. Alwyck's eyes reflected an inhuman hatred, and just as he lost his balance, the dark wizard grabbed Bruinen's robes and pulled his nemesis down into the dark chasm with him.

Kalleth gasped, and ran to the cliff side. "Uncle!" he cried, as he watched the two figures fighting even as they were swallowed up by the darkness. He slammed his fist down, oblivious to any pain. Rising from the ground, he surveyed the destruction all around. "The deed is done," Kalleth mumbled as he fell silent. His bleak expression deepened as he observed the details from the scene around him. Bodies with disfigured flesh where scattered everywhere, laying in puddles of slime. Kalleth shuddered and knelt beside Ezekiel checking for signs of life. A faint grin spread across Kalleth's face when he felt hot air warm his palm. "He's a fighter all right, but he requires a healer's skill to mend," Aeyri confessed. Kalleth looked up, "Verin?" he called out, searching for his cousin and spotting him standing next to Zarym Malic's body. Kalleth bent down to pick up Ezekiel, "A little help please?" He lifted his brother's significant weight with the goddess' help and walked quietly to his cousin's side.

Verin sensed his companions coming up behind him. He tuned everything else out of his mind. Seizing the opportunity to simply be with his father, as a father, and not the leader of the nether realm. "I must leave you now, please forgive my behaviour towards you, I was wrong to think of you as a failure. If not for the efforts of you and your companions, that scourge I once called my son would have brought destruction down on us all." His father's voice was barely a whisper when he continued, "Verin my son, shine a new light on our people, show them that there can be another path and lead them with more grace and tact than I ever did..." The dragon's head bowed as Zarym Malic passed into the great beyond. Verin bowed his head, whispering something to his father. Respectfully, Kalleth turned away from the half-blood who silently watched his father's body turn into ash and then gently blow away. Verin stood up his face covered in shock, "There's never any wind here! What's going on?" They both looked over at Bruinen's tree, and where surprised to see life blooming, and starting to spread. The pale grey shrubbery around them began to transform into vibrant green grass, swaying in the cool fresh wind. They gaped in amazement, seeing flowers bud, small forest creatures emerged and the brilliant sun, began to shine down. "Wow, what did he put in that tree?" Verin turned to see that Ezekiel had woken, and was smiling as he watched the expressions of wonder cross Kalleth's face. "I miss Bruinen already," Ezekiel sighed, still grinning even though the smile had not reached his eyes. Verin cleared his throat, and addressed the remaining soldiers, "This day dawned in bloodshed and though our journey towards victory has been a long and difficult one, we have finally emerged from this time of great turmoil. These realms are now headed into a new day of prosperity and possibility. Change is always uncomfortable at first and requires patience from all parties involved." He raised Ignaros, which gleamed in the sunlight. "But know this: we are finally free!" He turned to the captain, "Tend your wounded, and send out the scouts to spread the news of our victory!" The captain nodded his assent. Ezekiel groaned, trying to hide his injuries. Verin scanned the crowd and gestured to a six-armed demon, "You're a healer, aren't you? I need you over here." The medic snorted in derision and walked away. Verin didn't bother to hide his frustration. "Looks like I've got my work cut out for me," he muttered as he kneeled beside Ezekiel, "Never mind, I'll see to your healing myself."

Tereleth heard a loud bang as the door to her cell clanged opened. *Oh great,* she thought, *more of the horrible tasting gruel.* She was at a point were starvation was becoming the more pleasant option, but she knew she had to keep her strength up for the tiny life she was trying to protect. She was awaiting the same reptilian demon who had been feeding her for the last week or so. However, she was greatly surprised to hear a loud voice yell out. "The queen's in here!" A clanking noise soon followed, and strong, caring arms unwrapped the midnight rope that encased her. And so, after a week of being stuck in the dark, the first face that Tereleth saw was her knight in shining armour, at least metaphorically, because his armour was now scorched and dented, with a few missing pieces. They kissed, overjoyed to be reunited, and Ezekiel was the first to speak. "Why, why did you leave the castle?" he exclaimed. Tereleth laughed weakly, "To find you." Ezekiel looked at her with amazement. "What was so damn important that you had to- oh." He said, as he noticed the change to her stomach. "I-, When?" Tereleth simply smiled, "Sometime between when we got married and when you left, I suppose!" Ezekiel held his wife wordlessly, tears in his eyes. "What should we call him?" Tereleth asked. Ezekiel looked over at Kalleth, who had a bandaged arm and was smiling with Aeyri at his side, and Verin who leaned on the doorway, winking coyly. Ezekiel half-chuckled and half-sobbed, "We'll call him Bruinen, if it's a boy that is." Tereleth's eyes widened, "Wait, where is your uncle?" But when she saw Ezekiel's expression, she realized the truth and held him even tighter. Verin coughed, "I hate to break up this joyful reunion, I do. But do you want to leave the Netherworld or not? I mean there are great views of lava flows, bloodthirsty demons, and you can't go wrong with evil weapons, but I don't know if th-" Simultaneously, everyone yelled, "Yes!" And Verin held up his hands, "I'm just saying, once we commit there's no going back, I mean, let's consider the rep-" Ezekiel tenderly set Tereleth down on a chair and marched over to his cousin, grabbing him by the collar, "Message received?" Verin winked, and patted Ezekiel's head, "Yeah big loud and clear." With a snap they were teleported to the forest surrounding Bruinen's cabin. When Ezekiel finally let go of Verin, he grabbed the knight's arm. "Make sure you take good care of my niece or nephew and don't ever let that lady go," he gestured to Tereleth. "She's a fighter, that's for sure, and I'll be damned if she doesn't prove to be the best queen ever to rule Aetheria." Ezekiel smiled and approached Tereleth. He knelt down on one knee and placed her hand inside his own saying, "Let us get back to building a better realm, my darling. As ever, you remain the part of me which I cannot live without."

Tereleth smiled remembering the vows they had made to each other on top of their hill, "Yes, and may you continue to defend the kingdom with your unbreakable courage, greatest guardian of my heart."

Creaking leather and the smell of saddle soap always inspired a sense of adventure, Kalleth could feel his excitement building as he packed his horse with supplies. Verin handed Kalleth the mysterious ring he'd found in Svatan's courtyard. "Keep this ring close at hand," he said with a wink. "A simple circle, perhaps, but I believe this ring possesses untapped powers." Kalleth nodded. The cousins had spent several weeks staying at Bruinen's cabin to recuperate from their battle wounds and grief in equal measure. "You know," Kalleth gestured to the old cabin, "sometimes I swear I can still feel Bruinen at my side, even though I know he's not here." Verin grinned and slapped him on the back. "Farewell my friend, travel safely to wherever your odyssey leads!" Kalleth smiled back and hefting his pack up onto his mount, set out on his journey. Whatever the future might hold he knew, he would always remember this incredible time in his life. Contentment settled into his bones as he set off to explore the world outside the kingdom. However, as Kalleth passed beneath a great old oak tree, he stopped short, feeling a sort of presence enfold him. His horse nickered nervously, but when nothing more happened, he gave himself a shake for being silly and continued on. Kalleth hadn't noticed the slight lift of the oak tree's branches as he rode by, nor did he see the small carving at the base of the tree trunk which had been fondly inscribed with one word: *Bright-Talon*.

The End.

Epilogue:

That We Might Always Remember.

"Good night little Talon."

The History is Recorded

Ezekiel gazed pensively out the window of his study. He could feel the calming breeze whisper through the castle. Suddenly, the wind snuffed out the candle he had been using. The king had spent many summer evenings writing late into the night. Almost reverently, Ezekiel closed the leather bound tome for the last time; he sealed the cover of the book with hot wax and quickly embossed the seal with his gold ring. He smiled as he read the title aloud: *The Chronicles of Aetheria*. Feeling a sense of accomplishment and fatigue he quietly shelved the book and tiptoed back to his bedroom in an effort not to wake his beautiful wife Tereleth. However, one of the floorboards creaked loudly, and the king froze in place even as baby Bruinen stirred. He heard the first plaintive cry and then looked down into the crib, only to see his six month old son's face light up. The king hushed his son and begged him to be silent, but the baby would have none of his wishes. Over the past six months Ezekiel had learned many times that a mere babe could wield more authority than even the greatest of kings! Groaning in feigned annoyance and secretly smiling inside, Ezekiel lifted his tiny son into his arms and settled down onto the chaise for what remained of the eventide. "Good night little Talon."

CPSIA information can be obtained at www.ICGtesting.com
Printed in the USA
LVOW08*2003300314

379411LV00001B/3/P